Longir

A dog walker with a secret crush and a jilted fireman with no desire to risk watching his heart go up in flames ever again.

Fire Chief Brad Sinclair had his future planned and then his fiancée married someone else and left him and his heart in ashes. He's started over, seems to have picked up the pieces...but now his brother is getting married and his happy news is stirring up emotions Brad would rather he didn't feel. When the cute dog walker's apartment goes up in flames, he suddenly finds himself feeling the heat from attraction and the local ladies who think she's just what the local hero needs to put his life back on track.

Lulu Raintree is feeling mixed up and out of control— is she a stalker? She's been obsessed with the gorgeous Fire Chief ever since she moved to town. So much so that she sometimes hides behind bushes just to get a glimpse of him but she avoids coming face to face with him at all cost. When her apartment catches fire there is no place to hide as the handsome hero comes to her rescue.

But things are not as they seem and her past that sent her running to hide in the beautiful beach town of Sunset Bay might be the key to her infatuation with the handsome Brad Sinclair.

Heartaches are hard to get over, can love find a way to mend the broken hearted...and slightly obsessed?

LONGING FOR A HERO

Sunset Bay Romance, Book Two

DEBRA CLOPTON

Longing for a Hero

Copyright © 2019 Debra Clopton Parks

CHAPTER ONE

Lulu Raintree started out of the dog park, struggling to control Sebastian, a large, hairy, white beauty that was a mixture of breeds and a playful handful. She had just gotten the gate opened and stepped out onto the sidewalk when the all too familiar Jeep came into her view.

Fire Chief Brad Sinclair.

The instant she saw him in the driver's seat, her gaze locked onto him like a heat-seeking missile. He looked upset. As if her gaze drew his attention, he looked her way. She jumped back behind the bush, tripped over Sebastian, and toppled backward over him. She landed with a hard thud on the grass next to the concrete sidewalk, with her feet straight up in the air. Sebastian, thinking she was playing, pounced on her, dancing on her chest and barking as if he were king of the mountain.

"Sebastian." She laughed, mortified that Brad might have witnessed her clumsiness and grateful that the big brute of a dog had helped to cover her up so that now there was a chance that the gorgeous fire chief might not have seen her at all.

Pushing Sebastian off her and hugging him, she rolled to her knees and peeked to make sure the Jeep was long gone. It was. The coast was clear. Dusting herself off, she headed in the opposite direction from Brad. Sunset Bay wasn't a huge beach town, but like most, it was long and left ample room to avoid someone if you really wanted to. And she wanted to avoid the man who drove all her good sense out the window just by the mere essence of his presence.

Then again, there was the fact that she was a dog walker. At least, here in her new life in Sunset Bay, she was a dog walker. That hadn't always been the case. But as a dog walker, the fact that the dog park was across the street from the fire station did pose problems.

She was glad there hadn't been any other dog walkers in the park to witness her topple. She rubbed Sebastian on the head. "Okay, you really have a problem," she muttered. Sebastian turned his head and planted his big eyes on her. "Not you—me. I know you know it. I talk to you about it enough."

It was true. Her dogs were good listeners. No one else knew her history but she often found herself telling her doggy clients her troubles. Her fears and her hopes.

As she contemplated her life and in general her weirdness, Sebastian yanked and strained at the end of the leash the moment he spotted a squirrel. She had to leave her thoughts behind and hold onto the dog with all her might. He loved to chase squirrels and when the nearly sixty-pound pooch saw something he wanted, he went for it. Lulu was short, carried a few extra pounds on her hips and had a weakness for fresh baked muffins, so she had an ongoing battle with the scales and it was hard for her to sometimes keep up with the powerful single-minded dog.

Half the time, Sebastian drug her around town at the end of his leash instead of her walking him. It was no different this afternoon. As they were getting their walk in, she couldn't get Brad Sinclair off her mind. She had to do something about her reactions to the man.

What if someone had been watching her comedy act earlier when she saw him and then flipped backward over Sebastian and ended up on the ground? Rosie Olsen had spotted her hiding behind the Korney Korn truck during the town festival a couple of weeks ago. She saw Lulu peeking from behind the trailer but Rosie hadn't known what she was doing. She had wondered, though, and Lulu was sure Rosie had believed she was acting strange.

Of course, anyone would probably understand her actions if they knew it was Brad Sinclair who caused her reactions.

But that didn't change her confusion at those

reactions to him. Or how foolish she felt.

The man was a walking heartthrob and a heartache to her. Just the sight of him sent her heart slamming into her throat. Her knees had nearly buckled as she'd watched him pass by and, honestly, it was ridiculous that she, as a grown woman, felt the need to break out and run after his Jeep. Thankfully, she'd tripped over the dog instead.

The man drove her crazy. In a crazy way.

She had an almost unhealthy crush on him. She tried to avoid him at all costs because she was a bumbling klutz when he was around. So embarrassing.

Once, she'd had the unfortunate situation in a restaurant that she referred to as the great shrimp fiasco and could not bring herself to be anywhere around him where he would recognize her. And yet, she came to the dog park across from the firehouse every day to let the dogs run free and play. She hid behind the large bush in the dog park so she was out of view, and yet, she could glimpse him every day. A problem—big-time—yes, it was. And she wasn't sure how to fix it, because she didn't completely understand it. She'd moved to Sunset Bay to get over heartbreak…real, true heartbreak so why had she immediately become infatuated with Brad Sinclair? She just didn't understand her heart. Or herself for that matter. She had a problem and there was no denying the fact.

The salted air ruffled Fire Chief Brad Sinclair's hair and stung his eyes as, emergency lights flashing and siren screaming, he sped down the coastal road back toward Sunset Bay. He had been at his parents' home for dinner and not driven the red SUV supplied by the county. His personal vehicle was set up for him to respond to emergencies also and he'd wanted the open-air Jeep tonight. After his brother, Adam, had sprung a sudden engagement to the owner of Bake My Day bakery on the family, he'd needed the Jeep and the blast of fresh air as soon as he'd been able to wish them well and make his escape to the outskirts of town and a secluded stretch of beach. No sooner than he'd arrived Adam had called him, having seen him leave and looking upset. Something he hadn't wanted anyone to see. And then Adam had asked him to be best man.

Best man.

He was really happy for Adam, and he was now supposed to be his best man and he wasn't sure he could do it.

Just because two years ago the love of his life literally ripped his heart out and ran off to marry someone else didn't mean he was supposed to be brokenhearted for the rest of his life. But the way it was going, he feared he might be. Despite the fact that he hid it well with a lot of dates, a lot of smiling, and work, nothing seemed to ease his pain.

Work saved him. His work as fire chief was important. People counted on him. That kept him focused for the most part. It didn't cure the pain, the feelings of rejection, or fill the hole. But it helped.

As the plume of smoke in the air grew closer and the town came into view, he shoved the thoughts from his mind. He was almost there, meaning no room for thoughts of his past while he was working. His work required his full attention.

People counted on him and despite the fact that he'd suffered a letdown didn't mean he was letting anyone down.

About an hour after spotting Brad, Lulu was across town and still thinking about the man. Whether she wanted to or not. He was just there, stuck in her head. Taking up space she really didn't need him taking up.

He'd looked upset when he'd passed her earlier, though. What had been wrong with him?

She, like everyone in town, knew the story of his love for his childhood sweetheart and that they'd planned to marry and then she'd run off with someone else, leaving him brokenhearted—boy did she know how that felt. It was hard to see that the happy, dashing man who dated gorgeous women and rescued people from burning buildings sad. And she knew he was despite the brave face he showed the world. Of course, that was her take on him. He pretty much wore the red cape of a superhero where she was concerned. Just last week when she was walking Spaz and Sussi-Q the most terribly mannered terriers in the world, to put it in polite terms, she spotted him actually climbing a tree to save a kitty for a little girl. He had been completely adorable…the little girl had been too. But Brad, well he had stolen the show. She'd hidden behind Mr. Womack's plumbing truck and had been thankful that the terriers were trying to sniff out a mole that was tunneling a trail along the edge of the lawn. Her only problem had been when they found it and started straining at the end of their leashes and barking their cute little dirt covered heads off with excitement. Brad had been halfway down the tree with the kitty snuggled in his arms and had looked in her direction. She'd had to pick the pups up and make a dash for the edge of the house before he spotted her.

Yes, the man was a hero, and not just to kittens and little girls. He'd busted down a door to Mildred and Roland Birches home and he and Dex, one of the other firemen, had carried them out. That was just a few of the instances that he'd been a real life hero. But the truth was that he and the other firemen were ready to put their lives on the line to protect the people of this town from fire and disasters. And that was where the trouble for her started. There were plenty of heroes in town, from military veterans to firefighters to the police. There were more she was certain and the only one she had this infatuation with was Brad Sinclair.

She was biting her lip and letting Sebastian lead her as they passed the firehouse. It was quiet there and she'd kept her head down. She hadn't gone a hundred feet when the sirens sounded and she spotted the plume of smoke rising in the late afternoon sky toward her and Sebastian's apartments on the other side of town. Moments later, the largest of the three Sunset Bay firetrucks barreled down Seashell Lane and sent Sebastian into a fit of excitement. Yanking at his leash, the dog took off, chasing the firetruck and practically dragging her behind him. Of course, the firetrucks left them behind instantly but that didn't stop the dog from acting wildly out of control. Way out of control even for him.

She barely held onto the leash as she struggled to get her short legs to keep up with him. "Stop, Sebastian," she called. "Stop. Stay. Halt. *W-whoa*—"

She struggled block after block but the dog would not calm down.

She was winded but hanging on, running madly down the center lane of the oddly deserted street as the last block before her apartment complex came into view and she realized that was what was on fire.

Was the dog out of control because it had sensed it the moment the firetrucks went by?

Now, with the firetrucks and apartments and people standing around in sight, Sebastian completely lost it. She did too, and, gasping, pushed harder to follow along as they raced toward the fire.

The scene of the fire at Starfish Manor was chaotic as, sirens blaring, the backup pumper truck pulled to a halt next to Brad's Jeep. The first-floor apartment that had been engulfed in flames when they'd been called had been contained. He'd just come out from his initial look and he suspected an electrical problem had started the fire. No one had been in the apartment and his men were checking all the apartments to make sure

11

everyone was safe.

People swarmed everywhere, not knowing what to do. He'd gotten everyone to move back and barriers were put up as the men had gone into the burning building.

He was thankful the fire was contained to one floor and the call had come quickly so they could arrive before it had spread. Though the barrier was up, residents were worried as his men made sure the fire was contained. He was having a conversation with his hose man when suddenly a dog barking wildly drew his attention to the street. A large white dog barreled past the pumper truck, towing a small red-haired woman behind him. The woman clung to the dog's leash, yelling for the canine to stop. But it was doing no good. The dog was determined and had no intention of stopping until it reached its destination.

"That doesn't look so good." Dex Carpenter stepped to the side to stare.

Brad slapped his clipboard to Dex's chest. "Here, hold this. Someone needs to stop that runaway train." He could see the wide eyes on the redhead and knew

12

that the dog was leading her straight into the path of his men. Although the fire hadn't been anywhere near as bad as it could have been, he still didn't need this disaster getting in their way. Besides that, it was clear the woman needed help. That dog was almost as big as she was. He took six steps and intercepted the dog.

But it didn't go exactly as he'd planned. The massive dog dodged him, and the woman slammed into him; his arms wound around her and they both flew backward and hit the ground with a thud. Her gasp of pain registered as he took the hit on his back and she landed on top of him. And where the dog went was momentarily forgotten.

"I'll get the dog, Chief," Dex yelled as Brad lay sprawled across the grass with a mass of red hair covering his face and the fresh scent of fruity watermelon momentarily distracted him from the smell of smoke.

"Are you okay?" He felt her heart pounding against his, and liked the soft feel of her in his arms.

"I-I think," she stuttered. Her head lifted from his shoulder to reveal an oval-shaped face, with clear green eyes that stared at him with bewilderment through the threads of her auburn hair. In the seconds that their gazes locked, her gaze went from bewilderment to shock; then her pretty pink mouth opened and her eyes filled with horror. "It's you. Oh, no. Oh, I am so sorry." She scrambled to get off of him and when that didn't happen fast enough she pretty much crawled three feet away from him, muttering to herself then popping to her feet, all barely five feet of her.

From there she glared wide-eyed at him—pretty much as if she'd just had a run in with a snake or a skunk.

Stunned by her reaction to him, he'd released her and watched her frantic escape. Concerned for her and not sure what was going on he sat up. "Are you alright?" he asked, just as Dex showed up, holding the leash of the dog.

"Got him," Dex said.

The dog woofed and dove on top of Brad. One minute, he'd had an intriguing soft woman in his arms and the next, he had the hairy mass of a brute dog dancing all over him. And all while he was trying to figure out what had caused the look of horror on Green-eyes face. He'd seen her around town, just not close up very much. Once.

"No, Sebastian, no!" Green-eyes gasped. She reached to wrap her arms around the dog's neck and pull it off him.

Brad pushed and Dex pulled on the leash, and together they got the out-of-control animal off him long enough for Brad to get to a standing position.

From beyond the barrier, someone screamed the dog's name and came running up. It was a woman in her fifties, wearing a suit.

"Thank goodness, he's all right," she wailed, reaching them and throwing her arms around the dog. It instantly became a new dog and began wiggling happily in her arms. "There, there, baby. Mama's fine. I heard about the fire on my drive in from work and feared you could be inside the apartment with a raging fire." She looked up at Green-eyes. "I was so afraid, Lulu."

"It's okay, Ms. Gilmore. I—" She shot him a

glance from beneath shuttered eyelashes. Very long, cinnamon lashes. "I was walking him. He heard the sirens and we were close enough to the apartments to see the fire was here and he just took off. Drug me down the street as he tried to get to the apartments. I think he must have been coming to save you or something. He's chased squirrels before but never this. It's a wonder I held on." She grimaced. "Brad—I mean, Fire Chief Sinclair got in the way and I lost hold of him."

"Oh, you sweet dog, coming to rescue me. Thank you, Lulu. I'm forever grateful to you. Now, come on, Sebastian, let's go get out of the firemen's way so they can do their job."

Got in her way?

Dex looked at Brad and hefted a muscled shoulder. "I'll go check on the men's progress, Chief. Maybe you need to stay out of the way," he muttered and grinned.

"Thanks," Brad ground out, perplexed by the woman's reaction to him. He recognized her, having seen her walking dogs but she always seemed to be heading in a different direction than him. There were a few times he'd spotted her and thought she'd avoided him on purpose. But, other than her red hair, she really wasn't his type and he'd not had any desire to actively pursue anyone since Katie dropped him. He'd dated a lot but he'd never been the pursuer. So, there had been no desire on his part to actually wonder what the dog walker's problem with him was. Now, however, she stared at him as if he'd just tackled her and thrown her to the ground and trampled her. And he needed to understand why she had this reaction. "Did you say you live here?"

"Yes. I-I do live here. Is it bad?" She stepped away from him, still looking as if she were half afraid of him.

"We got here in time and were able to confine it to the one apartment. Number Four A."

Her eyes flew wide. "*Four A*—that's my apartment. H-how bad? What caused it? Oh no, it wasn't something I did, was it?"

"No, nothing you did. Looks like faulty wiring. These are old apartments."

She glanced around him and her mouth dropped open as she saw the blackened hole that had been her apartment. Windows were broken out and soot encased the brick.

"I'm sorry. Looks like it will be a total loss for you."

Her face fell. "Oh, I see." Instead of bursting into tears like most people did, she closed her mouth, seemed to suck in a deep breath and accept it. As if she was used to accepting bad information on a regular basis. She rubbed her forehead with two fingers. "Okay, I better let you get back to what you were doing. You don't need me getting in your way anymore than I already have. Hopefully no one else has much damage." Then, without waiting, she spun and hurried away.

He watched her disappear into the crowd. Her reaction baffled him. She was definitely different.

"Chief, we need you over here," one of his men called and he went back to work. He needed to get this figured out and then talk to the apartment owner. They were lucky this hadn't been worse but he needed an inspection to make sure the rest of the wiring was up to code or else they might not be so lucky next time. As it was, the dog walker was going to be out an apartment until hers was cleaned up. And she'd be very lucky if she salvaged anything. He hoped the complex had an extra apartment open.

Not his business. His business was putting out the fire, figuring out what started it, and making sure the place was safe going forward.

Still, as he headed back toward the burned-out apartment, his thoughts were with the baffling dog walker.

CHAPTER TWO

Dazed and fighting not to panic at the turn of events, Lulu stood to the side of the crowd, watching the firemen going in and out of her apartment, one of them was Brad. It looked awful. With its windows broken out and the dark singe around the window's brick, it was pretty depressing. From where she stood, it looked like a burned-up mess. *Her things…had anything survived?*

She nibbled her lip and berated herself because she hadn't taken out renter's insurance. Which meant she was homeless and had nothing but what she had in the bank to her name.

What was she going to do?

The only bright spot in her day was the fact that no one had been hurt and also that although she was a dog walker, she didn't own any dogs of her own. She just hadn't been able to bring herself to get another one after her sweet Bear had died right before she'd moved here. She'd loved that dog with all her heart and they'd been through a lot together. She still cried sometimes when she thought of him and had known that for now, she just couldn't open her heart to another dog of her own. Same with another man, but she was trying. Still, there was only so much she could take and adding another dog to the situation was more than she could take on. It just hurt too much when the end came.

She needed—wanted—a husband and a family. And though she had all these battling emotions carrying on inside her, she was pushing herself to try. Thus, she was half-heartedly dating.

"*Lulu*. Oh Lulu," Rosie Olsen called, hurrying to throw her arms around her and giving her a big hug. Then she stepped back. "Are you okay? I just spotted you here. You're so short I missed you in the crowd, though I'd been searching since I got here a few minutes ago. We were having dinner at Adam's parents' on the other side of town."

"Oh, that's good. Did you two announce that you were engaged?"

Rosie's brows knitted. "Yes, we did, and it was wonderful, but I'm here for you right now. Isn't that apartment they're coming in and out of yours?"

She nodded slowly. "Yes, honestly, I'm dazed at the moment. It looks like a total loss from here."

"Have you talked to Brad?"

"Um, for a moment. But I'm staying out of the firemen's way."

Rosie, ever the cheerful ray of sunshine placed a comforting hand on her arm. "Adam's over there making sure no one needs a doctor but maybe he'll know more when he comes back."

"Oh my *Lord*," Lila Peabody exclaimed, hustling up to them. "I just heard the news and rushed over here. Is the place going to burn to the ground? Are you all right, Lulu?"

"I'm fine and they have it contained," she assured the small lady. Lila was in her sixties and very active in the community, as were her friends, Birdie Carmichael, Doreen Posey, and Mami Desmond. As she thought about them, she could see the other ladies weaving their way through the crowd. The entire town was showing up, it seemed, as the crowd grew by the minute.

"Got here as soon as I heard," Birdie Carmichael said, scowling at the fire. "Looks like they got it contained. But someone's out an apartment."

"That would be Lulu," Rosie said.

"Oh no," Doreen gasped. "Honey, are you okay?" Doreen was a softie and even though Lulu was short, at five foot three, Doreen was barely five foot, if she was that. Even Lila was taller than Doreen. Birdie was small but still taller than Lulu, though she was thin and that made her seem taller than she was. Looking around at the ladies, she felt as if she were with her people because they all were below five and a half feet tall.

"This is not good, but..." Mami Desmond huffed

as she speed walked toward them. "…not good at all. Leave it to that *gorgeous* fire chief and his strong, manly fire team to get it put out before it did too much damage or harmed anyone. I just talked to Jim Mathews, the owner, and he told me it was your apartment that got destroyed. I am so, so sorry."

Mami was the vibrant, fourth friend of the group and towered above the others with her taller and fuller build. "He was a ball of nerves. Said he wasn't sure what he was going to do about you because he didn't have any apartments vacant."

Perfect. Lulu's mood plummeted more as her worry increased. *What was she going to do?* She felt faint and rubbed her temple. "It's okay," she managed, while trying not to completely lose it. "I'll figure something out."

"You can stay with me," Mami offered.

"Or me," Lila echoed.

"I have an extra room too," Doreen added.

"I might have a property available." Birdie looked thoughtful. "I need to check on a few things to make sure, but I'll let you know."

"I knew I picked this place as my home for a reason," Rosie said. "Everyone is so kind and helpful. You could always move in to my cottage with me. I don't have an extra bedroom but I have a comfy couch. Though that might not be the best thing if this turned into a long-term problem. But you are welcome to stay there as long as you need."

Warmth filled Lulu at their kindness. "Thank you all. I guess I at least need a place for tonight while I get things figured out."

"You'll stay with me." Mami took charge, helping her not have to choose between the ladies. That would have been a hard thing to do. "I have plenty of room in that big old house of mine."

"Okay. Thank you, all. I better go find Mr. Mathews and tell him where to find me if he needs me before the morning."

"I'll come with you, dear," Mami said.

Rosie patted her shoulder. "It's not much but I'm going to run to the shop and grab a bunch of muffins. I'll bring you back your favorite, fresh orange marmalade muffins. Everyone else might need a boost, too. Do you girls want to go help me?"

"Sure, we do." Birdie patted Lulu on the back. "You hang in there. It will be better tomorrow. You're going to be all right."

She gave a weak smile. She knew she would be, but right now she was overwhelmed.

Brad came out of the apartment just in time to see Lulu talking with the apartment manager. He couldn't help noticing she looked visibly shaken and pale with worry. He headed that way.

Mr. Mathews, who had his back to him, had started to walk away. "Mr. Mathews, I've given the okay for everyone to return to their apartments. The electrical problem appears to have been in a lamp and not the electrical wiring of the building."

The man turned back to him. "That's a relief. At least it's not bad wiring. I'll start letting everyone know. Again, I'm sorry about this, Lulu."

"It's not your fault," she told the man and, looking less than convinced, he headed off again.

"Have you found a place to stay?" Brad asked.

She nodded and was about to speak but Mami Desmond stood beside her and beat her to it.

"With me. This is terrible for Lulu, no matter what. But she's going to come stay with me until we figure out how long it's going to take to get her back in her apartment."

"That's good to know she has a place to stay." Brad tried to meet Lulu's gaze but she seemed determined not to look at him. "Would you like to take a look inside the apartment? I can take you in now, if you want." Her gaze flew to his and he was struck again by the spruce green of her eyes.

"That would be great. Maybe I can salvage a few things."

He wasn't sure about that. "Maybe, but I need to warn you that what wasn't burned was damaged by water. There may be some things in cabinets or drawers that made it through without burning but I can't promise it."

Her expression faltered and her eyes brightened with unshed tears for the first time. She sniffed. "I know. But, I still want to look."

Mami looked sympathetic. "I'll wait out here. Matter of fact, I see Rosie and the girls coming back with the muffins. I'll go see if I can help distribute anything. Come find me when you're ready. We may have to see if Lila or Rosie has something for you to sleep in because, honey, my clothes would swamp you." And with that, she spun and headed off, her flowing caftan flapping behind her like wings.

Brad watched Mami leave then looked back at Lulu. "She's good people."

Lulu smiled, and seemed to relax momentarily. "Yes, the town is full of them."

"Glad they are taking care of you."

She nodded and her gaze dug into his and rested for a moment on his lips.

The instant it happened, he felt a wave of awareness roll through him. *What was that?* Her eyes flared wide and she looked away but it left him staggered.

She wasn't his type, and then there was that weird way she seemed to blend in with her surroundings or spin and go the other way when he was near. Until today, he hadn't really thought much about her, except he suddenly remembered a few years ago when he'd sat down across from her at a restaurant and she'd had an unfortunate situation with a falling shrimp covered in red sauce. He had forgotten about that until now. He'd tried to help her just as his date had arrived and then she'd disappeared and not returned to her seat and a nearly full plate of food. That had been, what, two years ago? A while ago, but it was one more memory to underline the dog walker's odd tendencies that he had been aware of.

"Are you ready?" he asked, focusing on the now instead of that strange moment. He tried not to remember the shrimp episode. Remembering how mortified she'd looked as it hit her white shirt and splattered all over her before it slid down the slopes of her breasts leaving a trail of red sauce and then fell into her lap. He'd met her gaze and felt bad for her. And now that he'd remembered the incident, he wondered whether that had anything to do with why he seemed never to come face-to-face with her after that.

"I'm ready," she said.

He led the way to the door. Now that the team had cleared out, it was just the two of them as he led the way in. Normally, he would have let a woman enter before him but now, in this case, he needed to make sure she didn't hurt herself. There was fallen ceiling and charred furniture strewn around as they'd had to make sure no embers were still burning and had yanked the wet sheetrock from the ceiling and walls. They were soaked anyway.

She stopped in the doorway and gasped.

"Yeah, it looks bad."

"It is bad," she whispered.

He had the urge to give her a hug but didn't know her that well. "Yes, of course. Water damage does terrible things too. Have you called your insurance company yet?"

She ran a hand through her thick hair, drawing his attention to the bright tone. "I-I haven't."

"Well, do that. They'll want to come out and evaluate the damage. You'll probably have to catalogue your things for them."

She gazed around, looking lost, and didn't say anything.

"Maybe tomorrow you can come back and dig through it before the cleanup crews come in."

She picked up a photograph that was soot covered, the picture of her and a man. The photo was ruined. She stared at it for the longest time and then he saw a tear fall onto the soot. His heart ached for her. She suddenly seemed really alone.

She hugged the photo to her breast, not caring that the soot was rubbing off on her. He was a guy who usually knew how to handle most situations. He was good at interjecting humor into a situation but there was no humor in this—never was in a fire—but he was usually capable of easing people's stress in situations like this. He found as he stared at her, with her head bent and her hair cascading across her face like a shield, that he was at a loss.

"I'm sorry," he said, feeling the emptiness in the words.

She lifted her head and looked at him, pain in her eyes. "I have dogs to walk until about noon and then I have a break before my evening dog walking begins, so I'll come by then if I won't be in the way." She brushed dampness from beneath her eyes with one hand and left soot marks on both cheeks.

He remembered her shrimp and that she'd gotten so embarrassed and he was suddenly very protective of her. He didn't want her to walk outside with all those people and for them to see the soot marks. "You won't be in the way. It will take a few days for the insurance people to come in and for us to finish our review. Here—before you go, you have soot on your cheeks." He moved close to her and lifted his fingers, that he'd wiped clean earlier, and gently took her face between his hands. She froze as he used his thumbs to gently rub across her skin smoothing the soot from her cheeks. His throat went dry as her eyes locked with his and his stomach dipped. "There, that's better." He should have stepped back. Should have moved but he couldn't. "It's going to be okay," he said, thinking that her lips looked soft and he had the urge to lean down and see just how soft they were.

What was wrong with him?

He had encouraged many people and seen a lot of people in pain after losing their belongings and his heart always hurt for them. But he'd never stepped over the line or had the inclination to step over the line like he was doing right now.

He cleared his dry throat. "There, no more soot."

She swallowed hard then and backed away from him. "Okay, good. I need to go," she rasped then turned and hurried out of the apartment. Fled was more like it.

Brad rammed a hand through his hair then hung his head. *What had he done?*

CHAPTER THREE

L ulu lay in the fluffy pink room in Mami's house and stared up at the ceiling. The clock ticking on the bedside table sounded like a sledgehammer hitting a metal stake in the silent room. She'd been very well taken care of from the moment she'd rushed out of her pitiful apartment looking as upset as she was. Her home was gone, her things were gone, and when she'd picked up the ruined photo of her and Justin, she hadn't been able to hold back the tears. She'd only just recently been able to take it out of storage and put it on display, trying to come to terms with losing him. And now it was all ruined. All of her things, and his picture too.

She should know that it was just things; Justin's death taught her that. In this life, it wasn't what you had that mattered; it was the people. But seeing the ruined picture brought front and center that she had no people—only her mother and dad, and they were not happy with her at the moment.

Seeing the picture of her and Justin ruined like it had been had brought back so many hard memories. And then, Brad had looked at her with such tenderness. Her heart had flopped straight to her toes. And when he'd taken it a step further, completely taking her by surprise when he cupped her face with such tenderness she had stopped breathing. Stopped thinking of anything but his touch as he'd wiped the black smudges from her face. His beautiful eyes had melted into hers and she'd just frozen—stalled out. Lost herself in that moment.

For those few moments that he was touching her, everything faded to black except him and her, and his oh so gentle touch.

A touch that seemed surreal at first because she'd dreamed of it for so very, very long. But it had only been a dream of something she never truly believed would happen.

Never ever believed.

The clock ticked loudly, reminding her she needed to be sleeping and wasn't. She lay surrounded by ruffles and stared up at the ceiling lit by the reflection of the moon that was reflecting off the mirror and flickering like the old reels of a black-and-white movie being played on the overhead. Only tonight she saw those moments in her apartment replaying over and over again.

He'd touched her and his gaze had been so kind. So amazingly gentle as he'd smoothed the soot from her skin. In those moments, she'd lost all coherent thought and wanted to bury her face against his chest and feel his strong arms close around her and hold her tightly.

Wanted someone to lean on.

Thankfully, she'd come to her senses and was so bewildered by the look in his eyes that she'd jerked back and done the one thing she'd become very good at over the last few years—she'd run.

Needing to escape and put distance between the man she'd both adored from afar for two long years and feared too. The man who terrified her in so many ways it wasn't funny.

The man who probably thought she'd lost her marbles...the thing was, she'd already done that.

Around two years ago the moment she first saw his face.

She bit her lip and huffed out a breath of frustration. Maybe this was a good thing. Maybe this fire was the prod she needed to face her past and make some changes and move forward. She desperately needed to move forward.

She had the means to start over.

She wasn't destitute, though it seemed like it. She'd come to Sunset Bay and taken up a job with no stress involved. Thought that would help her find her way, help her let go. Instead of moving forward, she had stalled. She'd let the laid-back atmosphere of Sunset Bay and her low-keyed, no-stress dog walking job lull her into a place of complacency. And then the obsession with the fire chief had been a complicated distraction too.

It was time to remedy that and to also stop her obsession over Brad.

It was just weird and creepy.

And she was not a weird and creepy person.

At least she hadn't been, before.

Flopping to her stomach, she yanked her pillow over her head and groaned into the mattress. She couldn't run any longer and she knew it. She needed to decide where she was going from here. Rolling back over, she studied the flickering shadows on her ceiling and vowed that she was going to follow through, starting with decisions she made tomorrow and in the days to come.

She would.

It was time. Past time.

Brad arrived at the firehouse the morning after the fire at Starfish Manor. He'd had Lulu Raintree on his mind off and on ever since she'd spun and pretty much ran from her apartment and left him standing there in the ashes.

He'd found himself watching the streets for her as he'd driven into work but hadn't spotted her. Now, he stared out of his office window at the front of the firehouse to see whether he might spot her at the dog park.

Dex gave a knock to his open door and he looked from the window to wave him in. "What's up?"

"About the fundraiser. I'm heading up the fundraiser for the fire department and as boring as it sounds, we've decided to do a spaghetti supper again. It just makes more sense with the cost, and the return for the department can't be beat. People might be getting bored with it but once we crunched the numbers, it shows differently. They love spaghetti."

Distracted, he nodded. "Sure. Sounds good. What do you need from me? I'll support the effort any way you need me."

"Just help cooking the day of the event. And sell some raffle tickets and that's it, Chief. Volunteers are coming to help, too, and bringing desserts and side dishes. And decorating. I think your sister, Erin, is planning on getting friends here to help. She's doing a good job. Not sure if Cassie will be there or not. Doesn't seem Cassie is ever around anymore."

He and Dex didn't talk about Cassie much. Dex tried to hide the fact that he still held a flame for Brad's sister but Brad hadn't encouraged him. Cassie had a career in photography and was in high demand. She was not settling down any time soon and by all indications, she had no interest in Dex at all. He hated it for the guy, especially considering Brad thought very highly of his second-in-command. Dex was as good as they came. He just wasn't sure what had happened between him and Cassie that had caused her to avoid the guy as though he were contagious.

"You've done a good job getting this together. I can't keep up with Cassie's career or Tate's. Those two chose completely different life plans than I did. Hometown, small-town life is what I want. Hopping on an airplane all the time is the last thing I'd want to do."

Dex stared out the window and seemed to go

somewhere else for a moment. Then he shifted his weight from one foot to the other. "Yeah, me too. This is a great place to live, raise a family, and just enjoy. I don't get why anyone would want to leave."

"We have that in common." Brad thought of Katie. He tried really hard not to think of her but yesterday when Adam had announced he was getting married, it had brought back the memories that life as he'd planned it hadn't happened. "Well, if it's any consolation and gives you hope that there are good women who do want to settle here, Adam announced yesterday that he and Rosie are getting married."

Dex grinned. "No kidding. That's great. Rosie from Bake My Day, right? I saw her at the fire yesterday, handing out muffins."

"That's right. He's a lucky guy." And he was. Brad was happy for his older brother. And envious, too, and that was the truth of it. Adam was going to have the chance to have everything Brad had ever wanted: marriage to a small-town sweetheart and eventually a family to raise here in the beautiful, idyllic piece of heaven.

That had been his dream, but he would never have it now. Because he wasn't risking his heart with anyone.

Dex's expression grew serious. "Yeah, he is lucky. The woman has a special way with food. And coffee. Maybe I'll see if she'd be interested in helping with the fundraiser. Or you could ask her since she's about to be part of the family."

"Sure, I'll ask." He glanced out the window and saw a familiar small figure being walked by three dogs of various sizes. The big white hairy beast not being one of them. She quickly opened the gate and then slipped inside and disappeared behind the big, thick bush and out of his view.

"I, um, need to talk to the owner of the apartment that burned yesterday. She's across the road at the dog park. I'm there if you need me."

"Sure, sounds good. She looked real upset after you showed her the inside of the apartment. I saw her leaving and she looked like she'd been crying."

His gut twisted at the idea, even though he already knew she'd been upset. "She was. I want to find out how she's handling it today before she goes back over there after lunch."

"She's a nice person. My neighbor has her walk his dog, Oprah, while he's at work. And when he has to go out of town, she dog sits. Might be why she doesn't have a dog of her own. I always thought that was odd, you know, a dog walker without a dog. But then I was thinking about it after me and Mr. Winfrey were talking and I realized that if she had a dog, she might have to make arrangements for it when she was working. Anyway, whatever, she's nice."

Brad listened with interest. He had only been around her that one time briefly in the restaurant when she'd dropped the shrimp and then yesterday during the fire. He was still trying to figure out why they never ran into each other. Was she avoiding him?

Lulu had gotten up at her regular six a.m. glanced in the mirror at herself in the pink and white caftan that was several sizes too big and found Mami waiting in the kitchen, with coffee and a heavy breakfast of bacon and eggs, with homemade biscuits. *Homemade*, for crying out loud. She hadn't been expecting that and a heavy meal first thing in the morning was not something she ever did. Coffee and a muffin at Rosie's coffee shop was normal.

"Mami, you didn't have go to all this trouble. I've already put you out—"

"Nonsense. You are no trouble at all. You're going to need a good breakfast with all you'll have to do today. Facing the aftermath of the fire will be hard on you." Mami sighed. "I just hate it for you. And so does everyone in the community. I hate we didn't take time to find you something to sleep in other than my caftan. It swallows you right up."

"It was fine. You've been so kind to me, Mami. Everyone has. I'll be fine. Just fine."

"Yes, you will be. Now eat up, young lady, you need your strength."

Smiling Lulu picked up a biscuit and bit into it—it melted in her mouth. "This is fantastic," she mumbled and saw a smile of delight bloom across Mami's face.

"I'm so glad you like it."

The doorbell rang.

She clapped her hands and her eyes lit up. "Oh good. There they are."

Lulu watched Mami hurry out of the kitchen then heard talking and the sound of footsteps on the wooden floors. Several people were here it sounded like and then Rosie came into the room, smiling and carrying a small pink bag that was the signature color for Bake My Day. The logo was written across the bag in bright white letters. And she also carried a large blue duffel bag. Lila was with her, and so were Birdie and Doreen. They, too, each carried some kind of large bag.

"We came to check on you," Rosie announced. "And we knew you no longer had any clothes so we gathered a few things that we thought would help you get by until you can go pick out some things yourself." She set the duffel bag down and unzipped it to reveal colorful clothing and underwear inside.

"We had to make sure you were doing all right after the fire." Birdie set her bag down and it had shoes and clothing in it too.

Lila smiled. "I brought you shoes. I think you and

I wear the same size. A girl has to have some shoes. And I picked out my cutest shoes that I thought were your type."

"Since you won't fit into anything of mine without getting lost inside it," Doreen said with a smile. "I brought you some things that my neighbors all wanted to give you."

Lulu couldn't believe it. Tears started to stream down her face before it even registered that she was crying. "I can't believe you are all so kind. So generous. Thank you. I was just going to put on the same clothes I had on yesterday. This is so much better." She smiled through her tears. "What dear, dear people you are."

"You are too," Mami said. "But that's not all. Go ahead, Rosie—tell her."

Rosie smiled and set the Bake My Day bag on the table. "Last night while we were passing out muffins to everyone, they were all asking about how they could help you. And Birdie got the idea that they could give a little something to you to help you pick up a few things. And it was just the sweetest outpouring of love.

Everyone was excited to help. It's all there in that bag."

Everyone smiled as Lulu took them all in and then slowly opened the bag. It was full of money. It had been neatly stacked and Lulu gasped, her gaze flying back to meet the five pairs watching her. "This is too much. I have money. I can't take this from everyone."

"Nonsense," Birdie huffed. "You will take it. People generally want to help when something bad happens and it is the right thing to do. You can't steal the joy it gives them to help you by refusing."

"Oh, well, but—" She didn't know what to say.

Lila patted her shoulder. "It's okay, honey. Community is a marvelous thing. And Sunset Bay is the best community I know. Take it and do with it what you want. And later, pay it forward."

Doreen nodded gently. "Yes, pay it forward. Help someone else when the time comes."

She was just so touched, and overwhelmed. "Okay. But how can I thank them all?"

"A note in the paper perhaps would be good," Mami suggested.

"Yes, I'll do that." She stood then and gave each woman a hug. How could she have lost pretty much everything and feel as if she'd just gained so much?

An hour later, she was showered and wore clean underwear, bra, and a cute top and jeans that were almost a perfect fit—except for the length, which she folded up a few times so that they no longer scrunched up around her ankles. Her sparkly gold shoes Lila had given her were not her style but every time she looked down at them as she walked down the street, they made her smile.

She had a feeling that was exactly what Lila had wanted her to do.

She was just so touched by everyone's generosity. She was feeling upbeat when she'd thought she'd be feeling down. But the big-heartedness of this town had humbled her.

Her routine was off this morning. Normally, she had a cup of coffee from her coffeepot while she got ready to dog walk and then she stopped in at Rosie's place for a muffin and amazing coffee. And then she drank that as she drove across town and picked up her dogs from that side of town and walked them. Those early morning walks were too far away from the park so she walked them near their houses, thirty minutes each, and then by nine, she was back on this side of town, picking up her mid-morning dogs and making her rounds through town and the park. She had several dogs and did three dogs at a time for three hours and was normally finished by noon or not long after that. She started all over around two. If she wanted, she could work around the clock. She had a waiting list for if a slot ever opened up. In order to get them all in she would have to come up with a new idea for her business. Which she'd been thinking about but hadn't taken a chance on. She loved this town though and if she were going to do it this would be the place she would want to.

She shouldn't have been surprised by the town's giving heart because she already knew that Sunset Bay was a dog-loving community and that was a clue right there. When she'd come here and was looking for something to do to help pass the time and help her heal from all the pain of loss and regrets haunting her, she'd kind of fallen into dog walking by accident. Her neighbor was older and had recently fallen and broken her hip. Feeling sorry for both the neighbor and the dog, Lulu had offered to walk the dog for Ms. Carr. She missed Bear something fierce and thought walking Mrs. Carr's poodle would help the older woman but also help ease the ache in her own heart. She had enough aches in her heart without that of her poor dog.

Walking Jasmine got her out of the house, gave her a purpose each day, and the dog was wonderful and loved to be petted. Spending time with the dog helped Lulu. And then people saw her every day and within a month, she had a business going that grew from people seeing her out and about with different dogs and calling her or stopping her on the street to inquire about her services.

She'd been doing it ever since. And it gave her a legitimate reason to continue postponing going back into law.

To be honest, every time she thought about

walking back into a law office, she got sick to her stomach. She and her ex-fiancé had both worked at the same law firm and she'd been expected to walk back into the office like nothing wrong had happened. She couldn't do it and had resigned.

Dog walking had met a need but she'd decided during her sleepless night that it was time to make some decisions. She'd also decided to stop obsessing over the fire chief. But what was she doing right now? She was standing behind the big crepe myrtle bush, watching the firehouse for a glimpse of him while her three dogs played and romped in the fenced park.

And just as she was going to make herself turn away, he emerged from the building, looking strong and masculine and...determined.

And despite the bush between them, he seemed to be looking straight at her as he walked down the driveway of the firehouse and then crossed the street. Her heart thundered; she spun and looked for a way out. *He knew she was here and he was coming to talk to her.*

Calm down. He's coming to talk about the fire.

Not coming to confront you for coming here to stare at him every day for two years.

She heard the gate open and close and she closed her eyes and told herself to act normal. Not guilty.

"Lulu, how are you?"

She spun toward him, and hoped he couldn't hear her runaway heart pounding. "Hi. I just came to walk the dogs. See, they're having a good time."

He looked toward the dogs, who were chasing each other along the fence line. "Yeah, you come here a lot."

He knew. "Yes, I do."

"And, how are *you*? Not the dogs."

"Oh, fine. Just fine. I'm going over to dig through everything after this group of dogs. I moved my afternoon dogs to tomorrow so that I could get everything done. I didn't want to get filthy then have to rush to get them. Everyone was very understanding." She was rambling. One reason she was not a trial lawyer, but instead was a corporate lawyer: working behind the scenes for her employer fit her better.

He crossed his arms, drawing her attention to the

muscles and the strength in them. She tried to focus on his words, and not on his attributes.

"You were upset when you left yesterday. Are you going to be okay going in there today? Would you like some help?"

"Help? Oh, I think I want to go there by myself first and then if I see anything that needs to be taken out or can be salvaged, I might ask some of my friends to help. I honestly don't know that there is anything. It was so terrible yesterday."

"You might be right. Did you call your insurance company?"

"Okay, actually, I didn't say anything yesterday but I never purchased renter's insurance."

His lips flattened, but he didn't grimace. Instead, his words softened. "Oh, that's rough."

She liked that he didn't rub it in or act as if she were an idiot for not having done this. "It will be okay. It's just stuff and I have some money to start over. It was just...seeing my pictures and a few other sentimental items ruined that hurt the most. And just the shock over all of everything burning up. I'm not so dazed today."

She'd opened up a little because she didn't want him to think she had no means of surviving, because she did. She was lucky to have saved. And she hadn't brought anything with her, but had spent Friday mornings at garage sales and secondhand stores gathering furniture and items to give her apartment a lived-in, comfortable look. It had been another form of enjoyment and stress relief.

"Well, good to know. I just wanted to check and make sure you were coping okay. I see people who are emotionally devastated by fires, comparing it to deaths in the family. And I see people who recognize that if no one was hurt, then things can be replaced and life does go on. I'm glad to see you are in this category. It will be easier for you to cope. But either way, insurance does make the loss easier, so I'm glad you are okay despite not having purchased it."

She realized she was actually having a conversation with him without totally making herself look like an incompetent idiot. No freaking out. Her hard talk to herself might have paid off.

"Can I ask you something?"

She had looked away at the dogs, making sure they were still behaving nicely, and his question sent a shiver of dread through her. "Sure. Of course," she managed, wondering whether he'd noticed she was weird around him.

"I've seen you at a distance but only once up closer and the more I think about it, the more I'm thinking you've been avoiding me. Am I thinking clearly?"

She'd known this was coming. How did she tell him the real reason she avoided him? "No." She laughed guiltily. "Why would I do that?"

He studied her and she knew he didn't believe her. She was not a good liar and she didn't like lying. It wasn't in her nature. She'd become a lawyer to fight against injustice, even if it was behind the scenes. "Okay, you're right, I am a terrible liar. I have been avoiding you."

He looked at her with complete bafflement.

"Why? What did I ever do to you? I'm not a bad guy."

She wilted with embarrassment. "It's not you. It's me. I don't completely understand it myself. And that's the truth. I saw you once, and looked totally inept when I dropped a shrimp down my shirt."

"I remember that. I felt bad for you. I still don't get it."

"Look, I really don't want to talk about this. It's pretty personal."

That really had him looking at her with puzzlement, as if *she* were the puzzle with missing pieces. It bothered her because that was how she felt these days. She'd felt that way from the moment Tyson had stood her up. She was missing the super-sauce that made a man fall in love with her and stay with her. And there was the big possibility that another man would feel the same way…her stomach ached at the idea.

"I see," Brad said, finally. "Well, then, I'll leave you to it. If you need something that has to do with the fire, you know where to find me. Or how to avoid me.

Good luck."

And with that, he turned and walked away, leaving her standing there feeling like a total loser.

How could she tell him that she'd just gone through the most humiliating situation in her life with a man when she'd first moved here and she hadn't been the same since? Rejection on that level was a deeper wound than she might ever get over.

CHAPTER FOUR

Lulu had worn older clothes to walk dogs in and went straight from her last appointment to her apartment building. It was with a heavy heart that she parked her car and grabbed her new pair of gloves and then stared across the parking lot at the burned apartment. Taking a deep breath, she got out of the car. *She would do this.*

Her footsteps were slow and as heavy as her heart as she approached the building.

The meeting with Brad hadn't helped in any way and replayed in her head like a bad song that wouldn't go away. This infatuation with him, despite all she'd been through, still baffled her and obsessed her.

She had a problem; she just couldn't understand it or verbalize it. And it had begun the day she had been standing at the mirror, the happiest girl in the world in her wedding dress, about to walk down the aisle to her groom. Her pulse increased just remembering that moment. That moment in time, when all had been right in her world. That moment in time, just before things began to collapse.

She paused in the parking lot, staring across at the burned-out hull of her destroyed apartment, her heart thundering and instead saw her reflection in the mirror and the door behind her. The door opened and her mother had walked in. But instead of looking happy, she was as white as the beaded white wedding dress Lulu wore.

"Mom," Lulu had said, her stomach dropping to her strappy white heels. She'd turned to face her mother.

"Tyson is gone," she'd said. "And Suzanne is with him."

"What—" Lulu had said, halting as the words sank in.

"He left a note." Her mother had sounded as dazed as she'd looked.

Those words and his actions before that had changed her life. And then in the midst of dealing with that, her beloved brother had died.

And in the end, she'd run.

She was twenty feet from the burned-out shell of her apartment when her phone rang. She jumped at the sound, rocked from the past to the present in that instant. With shaking hands, she accepted the call without looking at the contact name and, as if her mother knew she was thinking about her, it was her voice on the other end of the line.

"Lulu, honey, I've been patient but I haven't heard from you in over a week. Are you okay? You know I worry about you."

She closed her eyes for a moment, gathering her thoughts. "Hi, Mom. I'm sorry, I've been busy. No excuse really, just busy." She really, really needed to let her parents into her world more. They worried about her but had been good about giving her the space she needed.

"Look, honey, I wish you would come home. I miss you so much and this is your home. I've tried to hold back and let you have your space. I understand that. I really do. But it's been long enough."

She closed her eyes as the world spun slightly. Her mom was talking about getting over being jilted at the altar, not losing her brother. Her brother's death was a deeper scar to all of them than what Tyson had done to her. And it was true...but together, it just left Lulu feeling as if she were on a boat about to be seasick. And now this fire.

It was time to be clear to her parents. "Mom, I know I've left you with the impression that I'm coming home. But I'm not. Sunset Bay is my home now. I can't come back there."

"But this is your home. And we need you close to us."

There was the guilt. "Oh Mom, I'm here for you. I promise I will start being more accessible. I'm coming to terms with everything. I promise. But I can't come home, not to live there permanently. Come visit me." The moment the words were out, she knew she really wanted them to come visit. "You and Dad need to come for a vacation. You'll love it here. But I can't and don't want to come home where I will run into Tyson and Suzanne all over town. Or have people constantly reminding me or feeling sorry for me about what happened. I cannot do that."

Her mother sighed. "It just makes me so furious that he did this to you and it messed up our family. You would still be here if Tyson hadn't hurt you."

Yes, it was true and she couldn't deny it. "I know, Mom, but we all have to face the fact that life is changed. I decided last night that I'm here to stay. I'm going to start looking for a house and begin setting down roots."

She had this problem with Brad but she wasn't going to let that run her off. It was time to face facts. The fact that she had been able to have a conversation with him this morning solidified that at least she didn't have to completely avoid him. She would get over being weird around him. She would. It was just some infatuation problem left over from the rejection of her ex-fiancé. She'd just had a deluge of bad things hit her at once and processing it all was what was weirding her out.

Car doors slamming and voices behind her caught her attention. She turned to the parking lot and her breath caught. Rosie Olsen, Mami, Birdie, Lila, Doreen, and Brad's sister, Erin, were all pulling trash cans, shovels, and plastic tubs from the back of a truck. They waved at her as they started across the parking lot.

The cavalry had arrived.

"Um, Mom, I need to go. I promise I'll call you later tonight or tomorrow. Okay. Love you."

"Well, okay, I'll be waiting."

"I will. Talk to you later," she said, a soft spot in her heart for her mother. But seeing this smiling group tromping determinedly toward her brought tears to her eyes. She was staying here in Sunset Bay for certain.

"We thought you could use a hand," Rosie called out. "We couldn't stay away and let you do this on your own."

"We certainly couldn't," Mami said. "We are here to help you salvage anything that is possibly salvageable."

"It's just terrible this happened to you and we had to let you know how much we adore you." Lila walked up and gave her a hug that made her happy and miss her mom at the same time. *Gee, my emotional state is just haywire.*

Doreen smiled sweetly. "I had a fire nearly thirty years ago and it's tough, but you do get through it. Makes you really know how little things mean, not that things aren't a comfort and help us nest and make places our own spaces. But, in the big picture, it's friends and family that matter. So here we are, determined to fill in the friend part."

"I'm so sorry, Doreen. I had no idea you had a fire. And I do see what you are saying." She didn't add that she'd learned that lesson already, through the loss of her beloved brother.

"My sweet hubby and I learned quickly the truth of it and then later when we realized we couldn't have children, it truly put our life in perspective." Doreen looked sad for a moment then waved a hand. "But enough about me. We are here ready to help."

"And I came too," Erin said. "We really haven't had a chance to get to know each other, but I just felt compelled to come and join in as soon as Rosie told me what they were planning. I've seen you busy with your dog walking ever since you came to town—we just haven't had that much opportunity to visit. But I hope we can fix that."

Lulu knew part of the reason they hadn't crossed paths was of her own doing because by avoiding Brad, she'd also avoided his family. Sunset Bay was small but there were several thousand people and it was a fairly spread-out town following along the beach line. It wasn't that hard to not know someone.

"I hope so. Thank you so much for coming," she said to Erin. And then looked at all of them. "I am speechless. Really, I am. This means so much to me. But, I don't think there is much in there."

"We'll find out together," Mami said.

"Yes, we will," Rosie agreed. "So, are you ready to lead the way?"

Lulu realized that she was. Having backup made it more bearable to walk inside and face the mess. She smiled, feeling bolstered. "I am."

Brad finished his paperwork, answered some phone calls about budgets and other business that he dealt with on a daily basis. By two o'clock, he needed a break from the office. He walked through the building where the fire crew on shift was hanging out, shooting some baskets at the back of the building. "I'm heading down to the dock and then may swing by Starfish Manor. I'll have my radio on."

"Yes sir, Chief."

Brad got in his official vehicle and glanced at the dog park even though he knew Lulu wasn't there. She would be over at her apartment, cleaning. He was still confused by her. Confused and trying to figure her out. Pulling out onto the road, he headed in the opposite direction of Starfish Manor and instead drove to Jonah's Boat Rentals.

Jonah was out on the dock and Brad saw him jump

into a boat, so he strode in that direction, past the large metal building that housed several different levels of boats whose owners rented space from Jonah. His brother had built a good business housing boats and then owning his own small fleet of boats that he rented out to weekly tourists or fishermen. He stayed busy but was very settled in his life.

Brad called his name and Jonah looked up from the motor he was checking out.

"Hey, Brad, come on in. I'm about to make a run and listen to the motor. Take a ride with me."

Just what Brad needed. "As long as it's not too far out. I'm on call."

"You got it."

He stepped into the boat and automatically walked to the front of the boat to release the rope when Jonah gave the go ahead. Jonah released the back rope then crossed to the driver's seat and gave him a nod. He'd already untied the rope; now he pushed off from the dock and moved to the passenger's seat behind the windshield.

"What's up?" Jonah asked over the loud roar of

the powerful motor. "You look like you've got something on your mind." Jonah's dark hair waved in the wind and his deep golden tan highlighted his vivid blue eyes as he shot him an inquiring look.

"Is it that apparent?" He shoved a hand through his own short hair, even though it wasn't long enough to get in his eyes. He stared out at the blue water as the boat cut through it with a steadily increasing speed. He stared at the horizon as the blue sky met the topaz water.

"It's real apparent. And you left Mom and Dad's pretty abruptly the other night. What's up?"

How was he supposed to say he was a jerk? He was happy for Adam; he was. But this had to do with Lulu Raintree. "Do you know the dog walker in town, Lulu Raintree?"

"I've seen her. She walks a lot of dogs. But I haven't ever met her. Why?"

He frowned into the wind as Jonah cut the boat through the waves and slowed the speed then turned the boat in a wide arc as he cocked his head, listening to the sound of the motor.

"She's been avoiding me ever since she came to town. I don't understand why. I can't figure out what would make her decide to purposefully go the other way if she sees me coming."

"That's odd. How do you know this?"

"She admitted it to me." He told him quickly about the fire and then going to check on her at the dog park. "She actually said she was avoiding me but when I asked her why she said it was personal and she didn't want to talk about it." Her words echoed through his mind: *I really don't want to talk about this. It's pretty personal.* "Am I that bad a guy that a woman would want to avoid me?"

Jonah looked as confused as Brad felt. "Man, I don't know. What did you do to her?"

"Nothing. I didn't know her until the fire. I saw her at a distance sometimes, but the woman obviously did a good job of avoiding me. I mean, she goes to the dog park across the street from my office and I barely even registered seeing her. And she has bright red hair, so she's pretty noticeable."

"Maybe that's it."

"What, that I didn't notice her?" He thought about it. "No, I don't think so. I saw her that time in the restaurant and tried to help her. And then my date came up and threw herself at me. When I untangled from Terry, Lulu had disappeared."

Jonah brought the boat to a halt and got up to check a few hoses attached to the motor. "I'm thinking," he said over his shoulder. Jonah was a man who used his hands to work, and to think. He'd always been like that, always busy. He stopped testing hoses. "Is she shy?"

"Maybe a little. She seems uncomfortable half the time she's talking to me."

"Look, I remember when I was younger, not so much these days, but when I was starting to date, if I liked a girl..." He grinned. "I could barely get my tongue to work right. I screwed up so many sentences. It was majorly embarrassing. Maybe she likes you. And maybe because she likes you she gets weird. And she can't talk about it because it is kind of weird."

Brad let that sink in. It felt like it could be what was going on. "Jonah, you might be right. Out of everything going through my head, this could be it. I can't imagine me causing her to do this, but it's the only thing that fits. Unless there is something I'm missing."

"You have been a serial dater since your breakup with Katie. Maybe that's intimidating too."

It was true. He'd tried to forget or prove that Katie leaving him like that hadn't hurt him to the core. Hadn't ripped his heart out and pushed him to the limits of not drowning in feeling sorry for himself. He'd given his whole heart to Katie, and her falling in love with someone else right under his nose while he was clueless, stung like a wicked giant scorpion strike to the heart. "I'm guilty. But, it's gotten old. I've just gone with the flow like an idiot—a good-natured, happy-go-lucky fella with no real depth." Depth meant opening up and he was never opening up again. But his curiosity about Lulu had him at least wondering what gave.

And he planned to find out.

CHAPTER FIVE

Carrying a box of garbage bags, Lulu walked into the apartment, overpowered by the stench of dampness, smoke, and fire. The scorched walls, blackened and burned out, were depressing. She studied the floor and stepped over the wet, burned sheetrock that had been the ceiling and now was a gross mess on the floor.

"Be careful coming in." She looked over her shoulder at the group and felt another surge of gratitude. She might fall apart in the next few minutes but maybe not. They might not have to know how affected she was by this but then they might and she realized she would be okay with that. These were her friends, and friends let friends in if things were too hard to handle.

"We will," Birdie said. "Lead the way, girlie."

She smiled at that, feeling fortified as she met the smiles from the group lined up behind Birdie. And then she turned and went inside. Her eyes landed on the photo of her and Justin. She went straight to it and picked it up. The rawness of losing her brother caused an ache deep in her gut. She had loved her brother so very much. They'd been connected like many twins, and when he'd died, it had felt as if a part of her was gone. She stared at the photo of Justin then clutched it to her breast as she moved onto her bedroom.

Pausing at the door, she looked back at her helpers. "I'll start in my bedroom."

"We'll dig around out here," Erin said as everyone spread out in the apartment.

She picked her way into the bedroom and stared at the ruined bed, half of it showing exposed mattress springs and half of it a blackened sooty mess. She hadn't made it this far last night; her emotions had overwhelmed her when she'd picked up the picture of her and Justin. And then Brad had cupped her face and she'd lost it.

"Here's a tub for you to store anything salvageable in and a garden claw to use for sifting through the piles and more garbage bags." Rosie set the tub inside the door. "I hope you're able to fill it up."

She set the photo in the tub then picked up the gardening tool Rosie had leaned against the doorframe. The three-pronged tool would work well on the piles of ash that had been her bedside tables. The wall between the bedroom and the kitchen was burned to charred wood where the fire had burned from the kitchen and into the bedroom. If the fire department hadn't arrived when they did, the rest of this room would have been burned far worse and the rest of the apartment house would have been damaged worse than a little smoke damage. The ceiling had been saved before the fire had endangered the apartment above her.

She used the tool to reach into the pile of ash that resembled an igloo made of ashes. She was startled when instead of pulling back a bunch of ash, the claw caught on something solid and the drawer front fell to the ground. What had appeared to be all ash was an illusion and there was a cavity inside. As amazing as it was, the wooden drawer had burned around the edges but hadn't had time to catch the insides completely on fire. Her heart leapt in her chest as she sank to her haunches and peered into the dark hull. A package of photos she'd developed lay inside. The last photos she'd had with Justin and her family. They were in her computer files and stored in her dropbox so most of them were safe, but just the fact that the tangible had survived clogged her throat and she pulled them out. Then she reached in the back of the drawer and pulled out the framed photo of her and Tyson. She stared at it. *Why had she kept this? A reminder of rejection of the worst kind?*

She knew there had been a few times when she'd been feeling sorry for herself she would pull it out and stare at it. Her head fuzzed up and she was baffled by her actions, as she so often was over the last couple of years.

"Are you okay?" Rosie spied her from where she was digging out pots from the lower cabinets of the kitchen.

Everyone seemed to be asking her that a lot lately—it was like back home after Tyson had walked out on her at the wedding. Everywhere she'd gone people asked her that. But that had been different because she'd felt humiliated and just wanted to forget it. "I'm fine." The words came out but she didn't mean them, she wasn't fine and she was fairly certain Rosie could tell she was not telling the whole truth. "I just realized I'd been holding onto something I should have thrown away a long time ago."

"Now is your chance."

It was true. "Yes, and I'm doing it now." She dropped the photo into a plastic bag and then picked up some smelly, wet charred sheetrock and dropped it on top of the picture. There was no time like the present to start not letting Tyson's decisions hurt her.

They pulled out a few things but by the end of two hours, she was carrying the large plastic container out of the bedroom, about to call it quits, when Brad tapped on the door. He stood in the doorway and she drank the man in as all of her insecurities rushed forward. She'd put Tyson in a trash bag but the insecurities left over from him had not gone inside the bag with him.

Brad had stayed away as long as he could. His duty as the fire chief and strong sense of responsibility overrode the knowledge that Lulu didn't want him here.

"How's it going?" Brad asked and was greeted with a chorus of women scattered through the room. They had soot on them, and looked hot. Lulu held a big plastic storage tub and he strode into the room. "Here, let me get that."

"It's okay, I have it." She held on when he went to take it from her.

He held on and met her with firm eyes. "I'll take it, Lulu."

She held his gaze, and bit her lip. "Thank you," she said, after a heartbeat, and let go.

Why was the woman so stubborn? So determined to avoid him at all costs?

Was it that she was attracted to him like Jonah suggested? He held her gaze as the buzz of attraction hummed through him. She flushed slightly and his interest in finding out what made this woman tick increased a hundred percent. "My pleasure." He hefted the box from her and an eyebrow at the same time. "I've held off coming to help you all afternoon and it just goes against my manly needs."

Birdie chuckled from where she held two garbage bags. "And we don't want to get in the way of you showing off those nice muscles of yours."

He laughed and joined in the teasing. "Now you're talking. If you'll put those bags down, I'll be right back to carry them out for you. Although the cleanup crews will come in and take care of this."

"I know, but we were sifting through everything and it just made sense to stuff unwanted trash into the bags. Helps keep things more organized."

"And gives us an excuse to watch you work." Mami grinned from across the room, where she and

Doreen were wiping soot off a couple of lamps.

"Brother dear, you have admirers." Erin laughed and he shot a couple of daggers at her for egging this on.

"They like your other brother too," Rosie told her, smiling at him.

Doreen blushed. "They are handsome. All of them."

Brad was starting to back toward the door, deciding he might not be teasing this group any more. They didn't need him egging them on either.

"Handsome, my foot. They are gorgeous. And we've been hoping you would come by," Lila drawled, her Southern upbringing sounding loud and clear. "Lulu needed the help of a strong man."

Lulu looked conflicted and was doing major damage on her lip. He had the sudden idea to bend down and kiss her lips, distracting her from hurting herself. Boy, would *that* give these ladies something to talk about.

"It took me a little while but I'm here now, and you ladies all look hot." They were definitely overheating in a bad way. "Maybe it's time to get outside where the breeze is at least moving around. Did you salvage anything from the wreckage?" It was time to refocus this conversation.

"A few things." Lulu sounded slightly breathless, and piqued his interest more.

Why did she sound that way?

She was the one person in the group he didn't mind finding him attractive. He hoped she did. "Good. I'm glad."

They all filed outside into the sunshine and where the soot was more visible across their cheeks and clothing. They looked as if they'd had a paint fight with black paintbrushes. They looked around at one another and saw what he saw, and immediately they all burst into laughter.

"You ladies look like you've been rolling around in there on soot piles." He grinned at them.

"It was a mess," Birdie said. "Worse than cleaning up after bad renters moved out."

Lila rubbed her cheeks. "I feel grimy but like I'm wearing war paint. We dove in together and got it done."

"Yes, we did." Lulu looked around at the ladies. "I never expected all of you to come and help me. I'm grateful and it feels so good to share this soot with all of you."

Erin, whom he hadn't even realized knew Lulu that well, crossed to her and hugged her. "We wanted to be here and I'm so glad we did. Now, like we talked about earlier, we are having lunch on Tuesday."

"I'll be there. I'll come as soon as I finish my morning dogs."

"I'll be there too," Rosie said. "We can talk about wedding plans too."

Her words reminded him again that soon Rosie would be his sister-in-law. She was a good gal and Adam was a lucky man.

"You girls need to make time to hang out together," Lila said. "We hang out for muffins at Rosie's every week and I always look forward to it. Girl connections are proven to help us gals be happy and healthy."

"I show up because they threaten me." Birdie

grunted.

Mami gave her a bump with her hip. "She is so full of it. She talks tough but she's usually the first one sitting at the table, waiting on the rest of us."

Behind her, Rosie nodded agreement with Mami.

Lulu glanced at him as the ladies started breaking up.

"Is your trunk open? I'll carry this to your car, while y'all finish up."

"Um, here you go." She dug her key from her jeans pocket and handed it to him. Her hand was warm as he took the keys and he smiled at her. "Thank you."

"My pleasure." He headed to the car and knew that for the first time in a very long time he was interested in someone. Truly interested.

"You like him," Rosie said as Lulu watched Brad walk toward her car.

Lulu tore her gaze from his wide shoulders, narrow hips, and a swagger that set her pulse racing. Of course, just the touch of his fingers as he'd taken the keys from her had started her pulse catapulting. "N—"

"Don't you dare deny it." Rosie's expression twisted in disbelief. "It's written all over your face. And besides, don't you think I noticed that you are completely not yourself when he's around? You clam up when he is around. And he was watching you, too."

"Yes, he was," Mami sang. "Reminded me of Adam watching Rosie."

Lulu was glad Birdie, Lila, and Doreen were busy gathering up tools. Erin turned their way, obviously having heard because the pretty blonde was smiling as she moved closer.

"I agree. My normally teasing and bold brother was very preoccupied, I think. And despite everyone talking to him, he could barely keep his eyes off you."

Lulu wished the man had stayed away. "He's the fire chief and I've had a fire. He's just doing his duty."

"Right. Keep telling yourself that." Erin laughed. "This is going to be interesting to watch. I've got to run. Time to make sure the B&B is ready for its new round of guests tomorrow. See you soon. And I'll want updates."

And then, as if a storm were suddenly blowing in and everyone needed to get to shelter, everyone told her good-bye and headed off toward their cars. Leaving her to face the handsome man who was closing her trunk and staring across the apartment yard at her. She shivered despite the heat of the day.

Butterflies lifted in her chest, an intriguing feeling mixed with a rising anxiety. With very mixed emotions, she started toward him, drawn to him as if pulled by a magnet. She knew this feeling, had felt it for two years since arriving here and seeing him. She still didn't understand how she could feel so inexplicably drawn to a man after what she had gone through.

Then again, she wasn't feeling all of this without anxiety. It was there, caught in her throat. *Could she believe the look in his eyes, that he was as drawn to her as she was to him?* It was a thought that she couldn't believe.

Couldn't trust.

Trusting was not an emotion she felt these days. It

was elusive.

"Would you have dinner with me?" he asked as soon as she got close.

Shock hit her at his invitation. "Dinner?" she asked, as if she didn't have the sense to understand the invitation. *She didn't understand the invitation.*

"You do eat, don't you?"

A soft laugh startled her; it shook with nervousness. "I-I do. But I'm a mess." She lifted a hand to absently push at the wayward strands of hair. Still unable to believe she and he stood here like this.

"Yes, you are." He frowned. "And I know that's bothering you, so I'm willing to delay the date until later tonight so you can clean up." He winked and she realized he was teasing, his expression a mixture of seriousness and gotcha.

"How nice of you." She laughed, a startled, instant response, and knew she couldn't get out of dinner with him. Her stomach rolled and a heat wave suddenly seemed to blow in on the salty air.

I just accepted a date with Brad Sinclair.

She honestly felt as though she might get sick. Not

a normal response to a hot date. She swayed.

His brows melted together and his gaze dug into her. "What's wrong? Are you okay?"

"I need to sit down."

He stepped forward and slid an arm around her waist. "Come on, let's get the car door opened." He reached for the door handle with his free hand and pulled it open, then carefully helped her sink into the seat.

Please don't throw up on him.

He sank down so that he squatted and looked into her face. His hands moved to her knees. "Do we need to lower your head or are you better?"

Her mouth was dry and the world spun a little but as she focused on him, everything steadied out. His hands were warm on her knees and a reassurance that he was there to help her if she needed him. Which was another contradiction to the emotions that Brad pulled from her. *Why did he have this effect on her?*

"I'm fine," she said, breathless.

He didn't look convinced. Suddenly, he lifted his right hand and gently pushed hair from her face. The little breath she had got stuck in her windpipe; the world stumbled to a stop as he seemed to stare straight into her soul.

Goal posts formed between his brows and his eyes probed hers. "Why do you have such a problem with me?"

She heard hurt in the resonance of his voice and saw shadows in his eyes, and she wanted to reassure him. She hadn't meant for him to think she didn't like him. They didn't move, but continued to stare at each other, and she knew she had to offer him some kind of explanation. One that she didn't completely understand herself.

"I'm sorry," she managed. "It's not you. I-I'm really not like this normally. I'm so confused." She groaned and looked down.

"With me you are. Something is wrong and I'm confused by it. I really try to be a nice guy."

"I know. It's honestly not you." She felt miserable.

"Then tell me what it is. Why have you been avoiding me? You say it is personal for you and you don't want to talk about it but it feels pretty personal to me too having a lady avoiding me. I'm not a bad guy. It bothers me that you do this. I don't understand what is going on—are you scared of me? Talk to me. I want to understand. I want to help you."

Thoughts and replies flooded her mind... She didn't know him. She *was* scared to know him, just not in the way he'd meant. "Maybe we just need to forget dinner."

"No, that is one thing we shouldn't forget."

She couldn't look away from him and fought to understand what was happening. Maybe it was time to just say it. "Okay, so, the truth is that I went through a really hard breakup before I moved here. And I'm a little weird from it. I'm not sure I'm ready to date." If the disasters she'd been on were any indication, then again, maybe it wasn't them but her.

Pain flickered in his eyes and it hit her that he knew what it felt like to be rejected by the person you love. "I'm sorry that happened. It must have been hard. I'm sorry you were hurt." She heard the understanding in his voice. Saw it in his eyes.

He'd known instantly that she'd been hurt. It was probably completely evident. She nodded and unexpected tears clogged her throat. She didn't want to hurt but somehow his quiet, comforting words *were* comforting to her. "Thanks," she managed, sniffing.

"It will get better," he said. "Little by little. At least, that's what everyone keeps telling me. Are you feeling better?"

"Yes. Truth is, I don't want to be hurt anymore by what he did."

"Sometimes that's not completely within our control. I think that dinner is exactly what we need. I want to—no, I need to understand why this is happening to you and why it's me who triggers it. Okay, can you do this?"

She nodded, knowing that this was absolutely what needed to happen. She had to stop stalking the guy and hiding out from him. She had to get past this craziness—if not for herself, at least for him. He had done nothing to get this oddness from her. "I'll go home and shower."

"And I'll pick you up at six. Is that good?"

"Yes, it is. And I'll try to act like a normal person when you get there."

"Now you're teasing me. Is there a normal person inside that pretty head of yours?"

"I know it's hard to believe but yes, there is."

"I want to get to know her. You're going to be okay to drive?"

"I'm fine. I'm not going to pass out now."

He patted her knee then rose. "If you did, I'd catch you."

It was a tempting thought. "I believe that."

"Then you've made my day." He pulled the door but paused before closing it. "You're at Mami's, right?"

"Yes, I am. She's going to talk. She won't be able to contain herself."

He smiled. "It's a small town—she would talk even if you weren't staying under her roof."

It was true. "You're right. I'll be ready."

He gave her a cocky grin. "See you then." He winked. And then after closing her door he walked away, that swagger of his holding her attention as she gripped the steering wheel with both hands and watched him walk to his truck.

I'm going out with him.

He opened the door to his truck, paused then looked across the parking lot at her and found her staring. He grinned broadly, sending eagle-sized butterflies diving in her chest. She ripped her fingers from the steering wheel and held her hand up in an awkward wave.

He did the same then climbed into his truck.

I'm going out with him.

Yes, she was. The man was seriously going to give her a heart attack. Taking a breath, she started her car, gulped in another breath, then drove out of the parking lot and headed toward Mami's.

She had a date with the sexiest man in Sunset Bay.

And she wasn't sure what to do about it.

CHAPTER SIX

"You're having a date with our hunky fire chief? Oh, my word, this is exciting. I need to call the gals and fill them in on this development. We thought you two needed to do this. They'll be as excited as I am."

"Wait, don't get too excited. I'm just going to dinner with him."

"I'll get excited if I want to. And Birdie would tan my hide if I didn't let her know."

Lulu sighed. "Okay, but don't blame me if you don't see what you're hoping to see."

Mami's expression turned to pure mischief. "Don't you worry about us. We're just excited."

That was the thing: she was excited too, but scared. She had been wanting to start dating again, knew she needed to. But was she really going out with Brad? The man who reminded her of everything that had rejected her a few years ago?

She was a glutton for punishment, obviously. The sound of a vehicle pulling into the driveway drew her gaze to the front window of the neat home that sat one street over from the beach at the far end of town from Starfish Manor. He was here.

I will not faint.

I will not act weird.

I will not run.

A knock sounded at the front door and she jumped.

Mami saw her and her hawk eyes widened knowingly. "He's just a man, coming to take you to dinner." She winked then hurried past Lulu and pulled the door open. "Hello, cutie. I had a feeling I was going to see you again."

"I've always thought you were a smart lady, but now I know you can also see the future."

Mami chuckled. "Oh, there was nothing mystical about me seeing this bit of the future. It was very clear to probably everyone today that you would be here—if not today, then soon."

Had they all been watching her and Brad like hawks in the little while that he'd been at her apartment or were they just all hopeful for some reason? Lulu wanted to know but didn't dare ask. "I guess we should go." She walked past Mami. Her knees were holding her up as she passed him, brushing his strong body on the way through the doorway. "See you later, Mami."

"Have a good evening," Mami cooed. "No rush. I'll leave the light on. I'll leave a pot of coffee on the burner for you too."

Lulu was mortified. As they made it to the truck and he held the door for her, his eyes danced with mirth.

"I'm sorry about that."

"No worries. Like we already knew, she was

excited."

"Just a little." Lulu was, too, as she watched him hurry around the Jeep and then climb in beside her. Moments later, they cruised down the street, the wind whizzing through her hair. She glanced over at Brad. He looked very much in his element, so strong and sure of himself as he drove.

"Do you like seafood?" He glanced at her and caught her staring at him.

"I do." She thought of the great shrimp fiasco. "I love shrimp."

He smiled at her. "And you look lovely wearing it."

She laughed. "Thank you. I'm going to try very hard not to wear it again."

"I didn't mind. You do whatever floats your boat." He took the road outside of town that forked down toward the beach road, and the town slowly disappeared behind them as the road wound slowly along the coast. She knew where he was going—a small restaurant that was off the beaten track but did a great business. It had a bar outside, with live music and a relaxed atmosphere.

"I love the Pirate Bar and Grill. The sunsets are amazing from there."

"I think so, too. That's why I thought we'd have our first date there. It's a very relaxed place, too. I'm hoping it will help ease your nerves."

She hoped with all her might it was that easy.

His words sank in. Our *first* date. *He had plans for there to be more.* She felt pressure building. *Would he still be thinking more dates after this one was finished?*

He whipped into the parking space and shut the Jeep off.

She started to unbuckle her seat belt but her fingers seemed stiff and she fumbled. Of course, she did!

He hopped from the Jeep and she was still struggling when he reached her side. "Having trouble?"

She yanked on the strap and pushed on the release button. "Yes. It won't release."

"Let me. It can be stubborn." He bent over her, his

arm touching her hip, his hand warm as he slid his beneath hers to work the seat belt release. She was instantly wrapped in his scent, a mild spicy cologne mixed with the undertones of freshly showered man. She studied his profile, stunned by being so near him. Frozen in pure bliss. And terror. *How was that possible?*

He chose that moment to pause and turn his head so he looked at her. "Are you breathing? Or holding your breath? I know CPR." He was teasing her and she let out the breath she hadn't even realized she was holding. She'd inhaled and must have been letting his amazing scent infuse throughout her being.

She was very thankful her weirdness about him hadn't come out and that she hadn't leaned forward and stuck her nose in his hair. "I'm breathing now."

He chuckled, deep and husky. "Good. I'm really glad you decided to come with me tonight."

"I am too." He was still leaning over her, his hand paused on the seat belt and his eyes warming her soul. "If the band plays loud enough, maybe we'll still be able to hear it from here, even with me stuck in the seat belt."

He chuckled again. She really liked the sound of his chuckle.

"I'm fine with that," he said. "But then we'd miss dinner and I think you're hungry, so I'll cut the strap if it comes down to that. I'm a first responder. I can get you out of this contraption. When the band starts playing, we will be sitting on that deck, watching that sunset."

She swallowed hard. "You're handy to have around." She didn't mention it but she thought she had the best seat in the house right now.

The seat belt clicked. "See, you're free." He straightened and the seat belt slid away from her as he held his hand out to her.

"Thanks." She bit her lip and slid her hand in his, feeling the warmth and strength of his big hand as it wrapped around hers. Shivers of awareness shot through her at his touch. She stepped from the Jeep and walked beside him to the restaurant. He didn't let go of her hand.

And she didn't want him to.

Brad had called ahead and gotten them to save his favorite seat at the back of the deck near the water. The evening was amazing and the sun had just started turning the sky a brilliant blend of golds and orange tinged with blue. He was determined to find out what was making this beautiful redhead tick. He'd been pleased when she'd agreed to join him, even though he had the feeling that she would have rather run in the other direction. *Why?* He planned to find out.

He held Lulu's hand, finding the feel of her small hand comforting and thrilling at the same time. He was confused by his attraction to her. She had stunningly bright auburn hair but other than that, she didn't remind him at all of Katie, or the type of woman he was normally attracted to. She was short, curvy, and appeared not to be very athletic. She walked dogs, but other than that, he got the feeling that climbing a rock wall or hiking more strenuous trails than the sidewalks of Sunset Bay might not be her definition of a good time.

But still, he found himself drawn to Lulu and very much attracted to her.

"Is this seat okay?" he asked as the hostess led them out onto the deck to the table he'd called ahead and requested.

"Perfect," she said, her eyes dancing as she slid into the seat he held out for her.

"Thanks," he said to the hostess and then he took his seat across from Lulu. As the waitress left, he cupped his hands on the table in front of him and smiled at his date. Jazz Nixon was playing tonight and the dude could play. "Jazz Nixon's music is always great. Have you heard him?"

"I've heard him once. I really enjoy his music. So island-time."

"Yeah, exactly. Makes you know you're at the beach and on island time. Very relaxing."

Jazz and his band had been getting their guitars ready and now started out with the tropical island version of "Somewhere Over the Rainbow."

"There you go. I'm relaxing already." She inhaled and cupped her hands on the table too.

He was very aware of her hands and had the urge to shift his so that he held hers. But he held back. He didn't want to move too fast but found himself for the first time in a really long time wanting to do more than just fill an evening with a companion rather than stay home. He wanted to actually get to know this woman. He decided looking at the menu was his best option to distract his hands from wanting to touch her. He picked it up and studied it.

"I can't get enough of their shrimp, so I'm not sure why I'm looking at this. What sounds good to you? Would you like an appetizer? I'm thinking some chips and dip would be nice to start with while we listen to music and talk. I'm not in any hurry to eat and go."

"I love their spinach and artichoke dip. But I think I'll steer clear of the shrimp. I'm going to go for the mahi-mahi fish and chips."

"Good choice. Though, are you sure no shrimp?"

"No shrimp." She laughed.

He was still smiling when the waitress came and took their food and drink order. "So, where did you move here from?"

She bit her lip, which he was starting to realize she did when she needed a moment to think before answering.

"I moved here from up north. I wanted to live near the beach. And this is a gorgeous one. I was always jealous of those who got to live on a beach on a daily basis rather than just visit it for a week out of the year."

"I get it. I can't understand why anyone would want to leave. Although, I enjoy going away for visits to other places but I like coming home to this." He scanned the blue water and white sandy beach. There were just enough clouds to make an amazing sunset. "Going to be a beautiful one tonight."

"Looks that way. What made you want to become the fire chief? What did you do before that?" she asked.

"I was a paramedic. And when Duke Hensley, the former fire chief, decided to retire, I had gone through a pretty rough patch myself and decided to run for the job. I guess I'm a glutton for punishment or something."

"You are very good at it from what I can see and from what everyone else says."

"I hope so. This is one job I wouldn't take if I hadn't thought I'd be good at it or could come through on. Too many people counting on me and my men." He meant it. He'd had to really think about it before he'd jumped, knowing the pressure that would be on him to do the job right. People's lives depended on them being there and being prepared.

"I believe that. I, well, I've seen you working." Her brow knitted and her pale skin turned rosy pink.

"You have? Funny, I don't see you around much at all." He was half teasing her about avoiding him.

She took a quick drink of her water, looking suddenly nervous. "N-no. I'm a dog walker. I'm everywhere."

He studied her. "Why do I make you so nervous?"

"It's not that—"

"It is. You're nervous right now. And today at

your apartment, you were too. Really nervous. I mean, I'm honestly very attracted to you but I'm not nervous. Can I assume you feel the same about me, only I am so amazing that it makes you a melting puddle of nerves?" He hitched a brow, teasing her. "And it makes you avoid me at all costs. Is that what the deal is?"

She laughed and seemed to relax a little. "So, you've figured me out."

"I'm trying. I'd like you to just be comfortable and be yourself." He wasn't going to push her.

"I'm trying." Her words were soft.

He did what he'd been wanting to do since they'd sat down—he covered her hands with his and gently rubbed his thumb over her palm. "Tell me about you. Why did you move here? I know you said you wanted to live on the beach but why Sunset Bay and why now? Was it because of the hard breakup you told me about?"

Her eyes shuttered and she looked away from him toward the band. He felt her hand tense beneath his and wondered why this question would bring this reaction. *Had the guy hurt her that deeply?*

"I didn't just go through a bad breakup. I was engaged and he stood me up at the church."

Memories flowed through him, memories he had relived so many times he couldn't count them. "I'm really sorry. The same thing happened to me, and I wouldn't wish that on anyone." He stared at her, feeling bad for her. "It's like being a member of a club you don't want to be in."

"Yes, exactly. It's embarrassing, hurtful, and emotionally debilitating all at the same time. And no one understands what you're going through. Except someone who has been through it." She blinked, and her eyes seemed to see him differently as she tilted her head and held his gaze.

He nodded, completely understanding what she was feeling. "And then you left?"

"Well, not at first but..." She paused. "A little later. I needed to put distance between me and him. And her. We all worked together. And then, my...after..." She paused there, looking lost.

He felt that, in that pause, she'd left a lot out. He decided not to push. "I guess you really have heard that you're better off than you would have been? I've heard it a hundred times at least. Honestly, I thought about moving myself after my fiancée called off the wedding. Might have been easier because I got sick of hearing them say that to me."

She looked relieved that he hadn't pressed her. "Yes, me too. I had quit my job. No way could I walk back into the law firm and pretend nothing had happened."

He felt really bad for her but then, despite hating it, but knowing it was true, he knew she was better off. "Why had you quit your job? Did you say law firm?"

"Yes. Because I was a lawyer in the same law firm as him and his new wife. And I refused to go into work and put myself through that every day. Besides, it just made everyone happier, me included. Later, after…well I couldn't stay and I came here."

"That's rough. Do you believe you're better off without him?"

"Yes, but I just didn't want all the reminders."

He couldn't figure out what kind of idiot had walked away from this woman. And he meant idiot. "Yeah, I know what you mean. I'm the same. And it makes me angry every time I have to agree with them.

Why is that?"

She blinked and looked out at the sea as the music continued to play the oldie "My Girl." He studied her profile and got the uneasy notion that she could be his girl. But he didn't want anyone to ever be his girl again. He refused to trust his happiness to anyone ever again.

Date, enjoy her company for a short while, and then move on. That was his way now.

Putting his heart in someone else's control...was never, ever going to be an option.

She suddenly looked straight at him. "I need to tell you something."

"Tell me." He held himself still to keep from scooting to the edge of his seat.

"I've been avoiding you. But there is more..."

"More?"

She took a deep breath and started to speak just as the food arrived.

He would have rather she kept talking.

CHAPTER SEVEN

What was she doing? Lulu had already confessed to Brad that she had been stalking him.

Well, *sort of* stalking him.

Which was so much more than just avoiding him. And made her seem so much more deranged.

But now she was going to tell the man that she needed to be straight with him about her heart. She'd been about to tell the man that she would never risk her heart again—not that she really believed he would ever truly fall for her…but she should warn him anyway. It was the right thing to do. Right?

But then if he was completely not into her then it was a silly thing to blurt out.

Thank goodness the food had arrived. Why would she want to confess something as ridiculous as that? He already thought she was a little strange. And yet, he'd been nothing but kind to her. Maybe she was totally misreading his kindness as more than it really was?

Maybe he'd covered her hand in comfort only. Even so, she might never wash this hand again.

The silly thought wasn't so silly after all as she looked at her hands tucked together in her lap as she waited for the plates of food to be set in front of them. She thought she could still feel the warmth of his hands wrapped around hers.

She could get used to this man.

Not.

"You were saying?" he prompted after the waiters had moved away and left them with hot plates of food in front of them and unfinished conversation hanging between them.

She picked up her fork and rubbed her thumb over the smooth metal of the handle like she would rub a worry rock. "I was saying, that…" She told herself not to make a fool of herself again. The man was having a momentary misjudgment. He would wake up tomorrow and realize that she was not his type and he would no longer be interested in her. She wouldn't see him much after this, as the fire department didn't have to keep checking up on victims after a fire. He had no reason to feel guilty or that she needed to confess her every action to the man. Why did she need him thinking she was odder than he already did?

"I haven't been on many dates since my ex, until recently. And those have been disasters. Thank you for inviting me, maybe this can be my first good date."

There; that was a true confession but not *the* confession.

He studied her, as if knowing she hadn't said what she had planned to say. "I'm a *great* first date." He grinned charmingly.

"I have to agree," she said, feeling shy again.

They dug into their food. It was delicious and after

a few bites and the good music surrounding them, she almost believed that there could be more. Almost.

"What will you do now? Are you going to stay at Mami's until your apartment is ready?"

She had just taken a bite of her salad and finished chewing, while contemplating his question. "Actually," she said at last. "I am toying with the idea of renting that small space across from the dog park on the other side of the road from the firehouse."

He looked confused. "That building on the end of the street next to the vacant lot?"

"Yes, that one."

"That's a sort of strange property for an apartment."

Her gaze went to the couples who were now moving to the small dance floor and swaying to the music. She was thinking of the building and of plans and as she looked back at Brad, she opened up more. "Yes, but I've been studying it for a while now and think it might meet my needs. I just couldn't make up my mind. I seem to have trouble making up my mind about a lot of things since I moved here...more, I should say, since I ran away from my previous life and relocated here. Do you know if it's up to code?"

"I'm not sure, but I can check it out. The owner of that place moved years ago after the building next to him, that he also owned, burned down. I think there had been some fraud going on with that building and the fire that it had. Speculation has it that he burned it down for the money. What would you do with it? Open a law office? I still can't get over the fact that you are a lawyer. I guess I've gotten to know you as a dog walker and that picture fits you better."

The idea had been languishing in her brain for a while now, but she'd had the thought that she might not stay, or that she'd get caught following Brad around and be so mortified that she'd run from town like she'd done before. Also, the thought of what her parents would say. She was a grown woman, still worried about what her parents would say about her choices. It had always been an ongoing battle that she'd waged with herself. Justin had always tried to get her to face up to them and do what she wanted, not what they expected. But it had always sounded so harsh. Her parents had only ever wanted the best for her. And she'd wanted to please them. And so she had gone to law school. Justin had always known the truth. Had always urged her to set herself free. But, despite his being right and free himself, she hadn't been able to do it.

Now, she realized, that none of those fears were hanging over her at this moment. "No, I wouldn't open a law office. I walked away from that not just because my ex and his new wife were in the same office, but because I never should have gone to law school in the first place. I felt out of place the entire time and a little like that character from *Legally Blonde*, except I was redheaded and never found my way like she did. I just managed to make it through by digging deep and trying to stay out of trouble."

"You are a puzzle, Lulu Raintree. No lawyer's office—then what?"

"I love helping people with their dogs. I love walking them, and I'd like to expand my services into a doggie daycare of sorts. I can still walk the dogs but would also have different play areas where the dogs can come and spend time with other dogs and run and play. And I can offer overnight lodging too. There will be kennels and indoor and outdoor areas. I can see it in my head but until now, I just haven't acted. My parents continue to believe I'm coming home and will resume my legal career. But I told my mother this morning that I wouldn't be coming home. I'm staying here. And I'm going to do this. There is a place on the second floor that could be a small apartment for me."

"I think that's a great idea. I'll check it out for you tomorrow."

"Thank you. Can I come with you?"

"Sure. I'll let you know what time as soon as I find out."

She couldn't help the goofy smile of delight that sprang to her lips. "Great." Her voice cracked with emotion. *This was what Justin had wanted her to feel.*

"Are you crying?"

She sniffed, and waved a hand. "No."

He was standing then and came to her. Before she knew what he was doing, he'd taken her hand and tugged her to her feet. Then, discreetly, he tucked her to him and moved them out onto the dance floor.

"No more crying on my watch," he said, close to her ear. "Why the tears?"

She was not crying any more. She was overwhelmed by being in his arms, of feeling his heart pounding just below her cheek. Her shortness made his chest the perfect place to rest her head. His arm was around her waist and his left hand held her hand close to his chest too. She looked up at him. "I was thinking about my brother. He died just a little over two years ago. Right before I moved here. I'm still not at peace with it. Probably never will be."

"I am so sorry. I had no idea."

"Not too many people know. It's too painful to talk about and I just have kept it to myself."

"He died very close to the time your fiancé walked out on you."

She nodded. "Yes, not long after that. It added to the blow."

Brad held her and his hand on her back gently moved in a sympathetic caress between her shoulder blades. It felt so good to have the comfort she found in his arms,

She looked up, drawing Brad's gaze. Their lips were close and he tenderly kissed her temple. She sighed. "He always told me dogs were my thing and that I should follow my passion. Not my parents' hopes and dreams for me. I miss him and I just suddenly get emotional sometimes."

"I can understand that. It seems like you had a lot happen before you moved here. A lot that would make anyone emotional."

"Yes."

He smiled gently at her and she felt it all the way to her toes.

"Despite what your brother wanted, I'm thinking going against your parents' wishes wasn't something that you could do either."

She realized it wasn't a question but a correct assessment from him about her. "Yes," she said, feeling a bit unsteady at how he seemed to know her. To understand her despite how little they knew of each other.

And she knew instinctively that she was treading

on dangerous waters. Brad Sinclair was not a man ready to settle down. She'd witnessed this for the last two years, understood it because she was the same. And yet, despite not ever planning to give her heart to another man, she had that desperate want, need, desire to have it all—the man of her dreams and the children she wanted to mother.

But wishing and having were two completely different matters.

CHAPTER EIGHT

The next morning, she woke and realized she hadn't called her mother back. It had been a busy day, going through the apartment with her friends and then when Brad had asked her out, she'd completely forgotten about calling her mother back. She'd practically forgotten her own name, for that matter.

Now, guilt rode in on a white horse and sat smack down on her chest. If she'd been walking Sebastian, she'd have sworn the dog had knocked her down and was trouncing her and she was dreaming she had a horse on her chest.

Whew, she needed coffee.

Dragging herself out of bed, she walked into the wall on the way to the bathroom to splash water on her face. She didn't always do well first thing in the morning. Coffee always helped on sleepless, restless nights. Because she slept like a restless toddler on a sugar high most of the time, she barely woke coherent. *Why was it that sleep always came fifteen minutes before the alarm went off?*

She splashed water on her face then shuffled to the kitchen to make her coffee. Only when she rounded the corner did she remember she was not in her own apartment but Mami's.

"Good morning, sunshine." Mami turned from the stove with a large smile that quickly faded. "Oh dear. Honey, you sit down and I'll pour you a cup of coffee right this minute. You look like you had a *very* late night last night."

Lulu had had a late night but it hadn't been with Brad. After sharing the dance with him, they'd finished their dinner and then he'd brought her home.

And she'd poured herself a cup of coffee that

Mami had left for them and she'd gone to her room to spend a sleepless night, going over plans for her new business.

It helped distract her from the problem of wanting to spend more time with Brad. But even the excitement bubbling up inside her at what she was about to do, of how pleased Justin would have been about what she was doing, nothing distracted her from thinking about how she'd felt wrapped in his arms. Of slow dancing with Brad as Jazz Nixon crooned the old song "Slow Dancing" while the moon glowed brightly on the water just a few yards away from the deck they danced on.

Mami wore a brightly colored caftan and it flowed around as she brought two cups of coffee over and set one down in front of Lulu and kept one for herself.

Lulu smiled up at the dear lady. "Thank you from the bottom of my heart." She wrapped both hands around the warm cup and let the warmth seep through her hands as she lifted it to her lips and sipped the delicious, bold brew.

"You're welcome. How are you doing? I have a feeling you aren't going to tell me any juicy news about your date last night. But is everything okay?"

"Everything is…okay. Have you ever had so much going on inside you that you thought you might bust wide open?"

"Oh honey, have I. You don't live nearly seventy years and not have a lot going on inside at some point." She took the stool next to Lulu. "Cream?"

"Yes, please." Lulu poured the cream into her coffee and Mami did the same. They both stirred the coffee. "That's how I feel right now."

"You know, you have friends. You could talk about whatever is bothering you. And I'm not talking about me. I'm here if you need to talk but you have Rosie too. And I think if you get to know Erin that she would make a good friend for you too. You are going to lunch with them on Tuesday, aren't you?"

Lulu took another drink of her coffee. "I am." She felt more human with every sip. Now that she knew she was going to stay here, the thought of expanding her friendships appealed to her. Until last night when she'd decided to set roots down here and actually open the business of her dreams, she hadn't realized how isolated she'd made herself.

"Good. Because don't think for one moment that I haven't noticed how much you seem to be missing for actual events this town holds. For instance, we are getting ready to help out with the annual fundraiser for the fire department. It will be a spaghetti dinner this year, which always does well. But I digress. What I was going to point out is that I thought about it and though you have lived here for two years now, you are noticeably absent from things like this. It is time that you start to get involved. I've taken the liberty of putting your name on the decorating committee and the cleanup crew. Same as me. Won't that be fun?"

Lulu stared at Mami. "But I don't do public festivals. And things."

"Well, now that you bring up the festival, I saw you peeking around the corner of the Korney Korn trailer when our handsome fire chief was having a conversation with his men on Main Street. And also, I saw you hiding behind the hat racks of the hat seller while he was buying muffins at Rosie's booth. *And* I've seen you a few other times trailing behind that man when he was out and about. How long have you been in love with our hunky fire chief?"

Lulu nearly spit her coffee out. Instead, to save herself doing that, she sucked in and it went down the wrong windpipe. She immediately started choking and wheezing.

Mami slapped her on the back. "Oh, I am so sorry, I didn't mean for you to hurt yourself."

"I-I don't love him. I barely know him." Lulu's eyes watered—from the choking and wheezing, not from wishing and wanting. *She did not love Brad.* She barely knew him. Infatuation was not love. She gulped her coffee then stood. "Mami, thank you so much for this. But I better get going. I'll take a cup and head to the shower then off to get my first doggy of the day."

"What about helping us? You are going to do that, right? After having a fire of your own, you know the value of the fire department."

She paused pouring fresh coffee into her cup. "Yes, I'll help. You can count on me."

That was one thing written in stone: if she said you could count on her, then she meant it...it was also the reason she didn't commit to too much stuff. Letting people down was not in her DNA. That was why walking away and letting her parents down had been so hard for her to do.

But when your world falls apart…it makes a woman take stock of her life in a whole new frame…and sometimes a new person emerges. One who has to be true to herself and not let that person down.

The thought hit Lulu as she was getting out of the shower.

She met her gaze in the mirror. Had that been what her brother had been trying to tell her? That she had to look out for herself sometimes? That it was okay to be reliable and all, but in the end she had to be reliable to herself or her house of cards could fall?

He'd loved cards and had built extravagant card houses, stacking them high and wide. It was amazing and she had many photos of him building those walls. And then tapping them and watching them fall. Her brother had always been stubborn and true to himself. Their parents had pushed for him to be a lawyer or a doctor like them. But he'd become a teacher.

And he'd loved every moment in the classroom with his kids. And they'd loved him. He'd had a gift of connection with students. And at his funeral, the place had been packed with an outpouring of kids and parents and friends.

She'd been numb at his funeral. In so much pain herself from losing him that she hadn't truly seen what he'd done. But now it was so clear to her.

He'd built card houses as examples of how not to build firm foundations. But in his own life, living by example and commitment, he'd built anything but a card house. His life had been true to himself and it made him happy and fulfilled in ways that she'd never known.

Tears streamed down her face. She grabbed a towel, buried her face in it and wept.

CHAPTER NINE

Sebastian was walking her when Brad called to say he had set up a time to check out the building for her. She checked her watch and realized it was in fifteen minutes. Feeling as though she were turning a sled around on the Alaskan tundra, she tugged hard on the leash and got his attention, pulling him back and getting him to head in the other direction. It was a workout for certain, but on the positive side, the dog helped her build muscles in her arms and thighs. That was a good thing.

Once turned around and his attention on reliving

every place they'd already passed, they were on their way. Speed up, slow down; speed up, slow down. It was like a heart healthy exercise: get that pulse up then let it rest. By the time they'd crossed town to the building, Brad was already there and she'd barely had time to worry about seeing him face-to-face again.

The instant Sebastian burst through the open door and practically dragged her inside, she was breathing hard. So when Brad spun from where he was looking at an electrical panel and his gaze met hers, there was hardly any place for her pounding pulse rate to go. Instead, her knees went to jelly and she grabbed a countertop to catch her breath.

"Are you okay?" he asked as Sebastian pounced on him, paws outstretched on his chest. He laughed at the dog. "You are a beast. And it looks like you've dragged your keeper through the wringer."

She nodded. "He's a workout and a half. Down, Sebastian." The dog looked over his shoulder at her and then complied, letting his paws drop back to the concrete floors. He sank to his haunches and stared lovingly up at Brad. Lulu sympathized wholeheartedly.

"Wow, the beast listened. But the other day at the fire, he was out of control."

She'd gathered her wits about her and straightened. "He was out of control. He was worried about his person. Dogs know things we don't know. Otherwise, he does take direction, most of the time. He just doesn't know how to slow down when he's on a mission. Or exploring. He's like a toddler. Which basically he is, just a really big one."

"I see." He grinned at her. "It's good to see you. He puts a lot of color in your cheeks."

Still holding the leash, her hands went to her cheeks. "I hadn't thought of that. I bet they are beet red. With my hair color, it doesn't take much to make me bloom red all over."

"I like it."

Instantly, she thought of all the red-haired women or various shades of the color that she'd seen him with over the last two years. In shape, athletic-looking redheaded women. She would say that the man had a definite type, but other than the hair and the pink skin, she didn't fit the athletic build, ability or inclination to be athletic.

That thought sent her pulse back to normal instantly. She better keep that in mind. It was good for her to remember that she was not the kind of woman he would fall for, not really. "So how is it looking?"

He didn't immediately reply but the skin around his eyes crinkled as his smile deepened. As if he knew she was changing the subject. *Drat the man, why was he so attractive?* In all respects, even that one.

"It's looking good so far. I've only been here about five minutes. If that. But the panel isn't overloaded and that's a very good thing. I like the building. It's been awhile since I was in here but I think with this concrete floor and the exposed brick and industrial-looking ceilings that this could be a cool place for you. And this door to the outside area works well too. You really did your homework." He had his hands on his hips and turned slowly as he talked, looking the room over.

She was staring at him, so when he turned back suddenly he caught her ogling him. She spun toward the doors and headed that way. "I tried. After all, it took me long enough to decide to do it. And spending so much time in the dog park staring at it gave me time to really envision it. But it was the fire that ultimately made me act on my vision." *And a big push from my brother.*

"Sometimes what we think is a bad thing turns out to be a good thing. You know what I mean?" His words were slightly husky.

She turned toward him getting the feeling he might have been talking about his fiancée leaving him at the altar. "Sometimes, but not always," she said, gathering her thoughts. "I can see that Tyson's leaving me at the altar was better than marrying me and then leaving me later. Good riddance. But I can't find any good in losing my brother. He had such a wonderful life, touched so many lives and died way too young. I can't find meaning in that."

"I'm sorry. I didn't mean it that way."

She pushed the door open and Sebastian ran through it as though his tail were on fire. She went unwillingly, towed like a large wrecker towing a bicycle.

"I know what you meant," she said, once outside and Sebastian was smelling the ground. "I'm sorry. I get grumpy sometimes. I know that death isn't for us to understand. It's not our timing that counts but God's. But, though I know this, I don't have to like it."

"True. Your brother sounds like he was a good guy."

Her heart twisted again, thinking about earlier that morning. "He was an amazing guy. I've had him on my mind all morning." She bit her lip, determined not to squall like she'd done that morning. "He would be happy with me. Very happy. He wanted me to do what I dreamed of. Not what others wanted me to do."

"I like him already. I take it, from our conversation last night, that your parents pushed you into a career you didn't want or clearly weren't suited for."

"Yes, but I could have said no. That was my own fault. Not theirs. They just wanted what they felt was right for me."

"You have a great attitude. I like it."

They stared at each other. They did a lot of that, as if trying to figure each other out. Trying to wrestle each other into slots that worked and keep them in line. She was having a hard time. She wanted to throw her arms around his neck and kiss the daylights out of him. She needed to do that. No, she didn't. What she needed to do was put him in that confined space allotted for friends only or business associates. She needed him behind a wall with a lead barrier that didn't let her hurting heart desperately long for him.

Because that was what it was doing.

Her heart was a traitor.

She didn't want to long for anyone.

Longing for someone was dangerous.

Longing for someone would get her heart broken. Even if it was for a hero like him.

A hero who saved the day for many in the community when the alarm bells rang.

Her alarm bells were clanging suddenly but she

would not let herself long for a hero.

Or anyone.

Those days were done. *Over. Finished.*

Thirty minutes after he'd walked into the building to check it out for Lulu, he walked out and watched her head off down the street, being towed by Sebastian, the great white beast. She was so small that she barely had the dog under control and walking so fast that her hips swayed in quick time and her long red hair kept up with it. She was a walking, delightful bundle of woman. Totally not his type.

Totally on his radar.

He actually loved that she was nothing like his ex or the other women he'd dated. Other than the hair color and he didn't even compare that to anyone. Her hair color was a coincidence and it was her own, uniquely her—just like she was unique.

And it was obvious that he bothered her. She continued to confuse him. He saw longing in her eyes, attraction, and even desire at times. All good things when it came to a man and a woman connecting. But it was the distancing and the strong hold she maintained on her composure around him that baffled him the most.

She was a curiosity that he was determined to figure out.

"Brad."

The sound of his brother calling his name had him pausing to look down the sidewalk. Adam was coming toward him. He hadn't seen or talked to him since the day of the fire.

"Hey, Adam, what's up?"

"I was picking up some supplies at the hardware store and saw you come out of that building and thought I'd say hi. I saw Lulu pass by, heading back through town as I was coming out. She laughed and said hi but that dog had her moving fast."

"Yeah, I don't think she has that one under as much control as she thinks she does. She's thinking of turning this building and the side yard section into a dog kennel slash daycare type place. Kind of a Doggie Bed and Breakfast."

Adam looked at the building. "That's a great idea. For the locals and the tourists."

"I think so too. Though I don't think she's shared that with a lot of people yet. I was just going over it for safety reasons."

Adam crossed his arms and nodded his head, looking thoughtful. "Sounds good. You sure it wasn't also in the *friend* capacity? She's nice. I heard through the grapevine, meaning Birdie and Mami and their crew telling Rosie, that you took Lulu out last night. Interesting."

He had known news would fly. Especially with Mami and her crew involved. "I guess Rosie hears a lot down at Bake My Day?"

"I think she does, but she doesn't share it all with me. Or a lot of people. She's all about taking it in if people need to share it but keeping it to herself and letting others do the sharing. But she was so excited about Lulu going out on a date with a great guy, as she called you, that she had to share it with me."

Rosie thought he was a great guy. The idea made him feel good. He tried to be and he wanted his future sister-in-law to like him. "Lulu doesn't normally date great guys? And I like that Rosie thinks highly of me. She's a great gal. You are a lucky man." It was true. He realized his stress over Adam and Rosie's engagement had eased. The tension and jealousy he'd felt was barely there.

Adam's brows crinkled above serious eyes. "I'm glad you think so. We want you to be happy for us and we want you to be happy. I know it takes awhile to sometimes get over deep hurts and, well, anyway, I'm glad you like Rosie. She likes you. And she says Lulu had confessed that her dating life has been tough."

"Does she know much about Lulu's life before she came here?"

"I don't think so. I think Lulu is a bit of a mystery. Rosie had her own history before she came here, so she respects people's need to share their history when they feel comfortable. I don't think Lulu is there yet. Rosie isn't either. Nothing bad—it's just personal. I had my own struggle with that. I need to go but I'll share it with you in the near future. I know you of all people understand all about why it's good to keep some things to yourself and that there is a time to open up and a time to hold things close."

"Boy, don't I know it. I live my history in living color, with everyone in town knowing it. And everyone in town continually asking me how I'm doing and when am I going to move on and settle down. It's really not something I'd wish on anyone, so believe me—I respect everyone's right to privacy."

Adam clamped a hand on his shoulder. "I hear you, so I won't ask."

Brad laughed again. "I'm fine, big brother. I'm actually doing better every day."

"Good to know. Talk to you later."

He watched Adam head to his truck. Brad realized what he'd said was true. He was doing better every day.

Strange how only a few days ago he wouldn't have said that. Only a few days ago, he'd been standing by the water's edge, wanting to shout at the world.

What was up with that?

CHAPTER TEN

Tuesday morning, Lulu met Rosie and Erin at Bake My Day. It was the best place to meet because Rosie didn't have a car, preferring to ride her bike around town. They had decided they'd meet there then head out from there for lunch since the bakery was not the best place for them to have lunch because Rosie would be visiting with everyone who came in. They piled into Erin's small SUV and headed toward a café at the far edge of town that was frequented by more tourists than locals. It also had a nice deck with a great view.

Lulu had been touched that morning by how excited Mami was about her and "the young gals" as she had labeled them, considering her and her group she called "the old gals", getting together. She talked about how her and the old gals had all met while "snowbirding" here in Sunset Bay, living here only in the cold months of the various home states and moving here and then heading back during the hotter months of summer. Then, after they'd all had enough of the moving back and forth, they had all decided to relocate around the same time and call the beautiful town their own. Lulu felt a kindred spirit to them in some ways. And now Mami was thrilled that she was forming friendships.

Lulu was too. And it was another beautiful day in the neighborhood, with the sun shining and the blue sky dotted with vivid white clouds that cast small shadows on various areas of the glistening topaz waters lapping at the white sand. Sometimes she needed to pinch herself, this place was so beautiful and she lived here.

"Have you made any plans since the fire?" Erin

asked after they'd gotten settled and had made small talk about how excited they all were to get to know one another.

Lulu was glad to know she wasn't the only one happy about the lunch and the possibilities. Though she was curious about why Erin was so excited. After all, she'd grown up here and probably had a lot of friends in town.

"I have, actually. I mean, I am so grateful for Mami and for everyone stepping in to rescue me but I've just rented that vacant building across from the dog park and the vacant lot next to it. I'm opening a doggy daycare/kennel. And there is an apartment upstairs that comes with it. I move in this weekend."

"Seriously, that is wonderful," Rosie exclaimed, jumping from her chair to throw her arms around Lulu.

This made Lulu laugh with joy.

Joy. It was a word she hadn't used in forever.

Erin was laughing, too, and delight shone on her face, her blue eyes dancing. "I agree with Rosie. It is amazing." She reached out, grasped Lulu's forearm and gave it a gentle squeeze. "I'm thrilled for you."

Rosie sat back down, still smiling. "A doggy daycare. It fits you."

Lulu felt suddenly self-conscious. "Actually, it does. See, before I came here, I was a miserable lawyer. Not that lawyers are miserable people but it was how I felt. And then, well, I went through getting dumped at the altar…and I lost my brother. He died in a car crash. And then, as if nothing else could go wrong, my dog died on me too." She got the entire story out without crying. Her heart hurt but she managed to hold it all together. Opening up to Brad had helped her. She'd held it all in for so long. "I'm not telling you this to make you feel sorry for me. I'm just saying I had a hard year right before I decided to move here. And I walked away from everything." And as they sat there, she let her story out and she felt a freedom in opening up to these two.

Rosie—always happy, always a ray of sunshine—suddenly grew serious. "As long as we're sharing, I've only told this to Adam but I almost died before coming here. I had a rare form of cancer and was blessed with a second chance at life. I chose to start over here.

Sitting here, I realized that in not sharing my past with you, if we are indeed forming a bond, that it was almost impossible for me to really do that without sharing that part of my life. I don't want it shared everywhere, please, but it's nice opening up."

Lulu couldn't believe it. "Rosie, I would never have guessed that you had gone through something like that. I'm so glad you survived."

Rosie smiled. "And I'm glad you survived. Maybe it was a little different but we both went through the fire and came out on the other side."

Lulu let that sink in. "Yes, we did."

"You both amaze me. I'm so glad we're getting together and I have to confess, I'm thrilled Rosie and Adam are getting married. He needed someone so badly. And Lulu, Brad seems to actually be engaged when you are around."

"Engaged?" Lulu did not understand.

Erin bopped herself on the forehead with two fingers. "Not engaged as engaged. I mean, actively participating. Engaged in the actual conversation, the interaction you and he are having. That day at your apartment he seemed a bit off-kilter—you know, the way a man can be when he's attracted and testing the waters. I was so hoping he would ask you out and he did. And I heard through the grapevine, not Mami and her gals, but one of the waitresses there helps out at the B&B sometimes and she saw you two dancing and looking very seriously connected, as she put it."

Lulu let that sink in. They had been seriously connected as he'd used the dancing as an excuse to hold her and console her. Just thinking about it caused butterflies to rise in her chest. But that needed to be kept to herself. "He's a nice guy. We both have had issues with people we trusted rejecting us. We talked about that some. And…he's a really good dancer." There, she'd said something without completely giving away her warped feelings.

"I think you have more than that connecting you," Rosie said, her voice soft and encouraging. "He looks at you like you're the best thing ever."

"The deal is," Erin said, sighing, "he looks at you. Really looks at you. He hasn't done that since Katie. After she hurt him it's been like he turned on the charm and pulled down the shutters on his eyes—you know, the windows to his soul."

Just the words sent an unwelcome thrill through her. *Was it true? Could it be that Brad really hadn't been truly interested in the other women he dated? All those gorgeous women? Could she really stand a chance with him?*

The idea didn't seem possible. And yet, it sent hope through her.

But she didn't want that. She couldn't ever let herself want or need a man.

"Don't look so scared." Erin took a bite of the shrimp scampi. "I promise I'm just making an observation and from one woman to another, I thought it was information you might need to know."

She stored that away to pull out and think about later. *Did she truly believe he looked at her differently than he'd looked at the long list of women he'd dated since she'd come to town?*

Did she want him to look at her differently?

"Looks like you're going to have a good turnout. You certainly have a great volunteer group," Jonah said, standing beside Brad as they watched people hustling around everywhere getting things ready for the fundraiser.

Brad stared at the firehouse with the tables all set out where the trucks were usually parked. They were on the street, one blocking traffic on one end of the street and one blocking access from the other end of the street. The area between was protected from cars entering and everyone could roam and enjoy the festivities safely. There would be games for the kids, such as ring toss and climb the pole and—his favorite—who can put on the fireman suit the quickest. There were tables here too, plenty of seating for the locals who came out in support of the fire station. His gaze snagged on Lulu as she used a helium tank to air up balloons. Birdie was helping her, more like telling her how to do it and Lulu was grinning. Looking at her his heart felt lighter just seeing her smiling face. She seemed to have that effect on him.

He and his brothers had been busy getting tables and chairs set up all around. So though he'd been talking to everyone in spurts there hadn't been any time to spend time with her. But he planned on doing that before the night was over.

"Hey, Chief, want to taste the sauce?" Dex called. He and Maverick Hensworth were in charge of the sauce. If the sauce wasn't good, then the night was ruined as far as food went. Dex and Maverick were the best cooks of all the firemen, so they had taken on the responsibility of cooking the main dish.

"Nope, you know you can handle that."

"Okay, but really, I just wanted to hear you tell me how good it is." Dex chuckled.

"You know mine's better." Maverick elbowed Dex in the ribs.

"Here, we'll taste it," Mami said from where she'd been setting out veggie plates.

"We certainly will," Lila agreed and the two swept across the concrete drive in a flash.

"And it better be good," Mami declared, grinning broadly at the two firemen.

"I'll test it, too," Birdie snapped. "You might need a little advice on spicing it up." She hurried his way and handed him the balloon she'd been about to fill up. "You can take over for me."

"I believe you boys are in good hands," he called to Maverick and Dex. Then, glad to take up the task, he asked Adam and Jonah, "You two got this?"

"I believe we can handle it," Adam said, with more than a little laughter in his voice.

"The question is can you handle the balloon duty?" Jonah asked, for his ears only.

He looked at his brothers, saw clearly that they knew what he was doing and realized that he had no problem with anyone assuming he was interested in Lulu. He headed toward her, with thundering heart.

Those two had their hands full now. They'd probably be adding a pinch of this and a pinch of that until people started to arrive.

He saw Rosie pull up in Adam's truck and Adam headed toward her. She was bringing muffins for the event, something he personally was grateful for because he loved Bake My Day muffins. Especially the orange-cinnamon and the orange marmalade ones.

"Hey," he said, once he reached Lulu. He jiggled the red balloon he held. "You have a lot of balloons blown up, but now the A team is here to help."

147

"Oh, full of yourself, aren't you?"

"No, just trying to impress the lady."

She smiled. "Then by all means jump in here and show me what you've got. I love balloons."

He sank onto the bench across from her so the helium container was between them. "I bet you always had them tied to your wrist at festivals." He filled the red balloon up as he spoke.

"Yes, I did," she gasped. "How did you guess?"

"I just had this sudden vision of a cute little redheaded girl with a bunch of balloons."

"That was me. I always thought it was fun to have a bunch of them tied to my wrist. My mom liked it because it helped her keep up with me."

"I bet you were a cute little kid. I'm surprised you didn't have a puppy in your arms too."

She tilted her head, the look in her eyes told him he'd just nailed another childhood tendency of hers. "Yes," she said. "You seem to have me all figured out."

His heart thundered in his chest as memories of holding her while they'd danced filled his mind. He'd had her on his mind pretty much constantly these last few days. He'd been busy with putting out fires—small ones here and there—and then dealing with budgets and more paperwork than he was happy about but at the end of the month he had to get it done. He hadn't ever been one to look forward to the fundraisers like the other guys did, but he'd been more than excited to be here tonight because he knew Lulu would be here.

"I'm trying," he said, softly.

She inhaled then busied herself filling a balloon. "I was a precocious little kid. Always running away to find puppies and frightening years off my parents when they had to frantically search for me. My brother always knew where to find me, though." She stopped what she was doing. "I want to thank you again for putting up with my emotions the other night."

He gently traced a finger along her wrist. "No need to thank me. I'm glad I could be there for you."

"You were. And it's been a while since anyone was, at least like that."

"Well, to be honest, it was completely personal on my part. I wanted to be there for you." He let his fingers rest on her wrist as her gaze dropped to his fingers and he saw her slight shiver and knew she felt it, too. "Would you go out with me again?"

Her gaze lifted slowly to his. "Brad, I'm not sure this is a good idea. We both, well, we both admitted that we're not ready for or wanting long-term relationships."

"Why don't we take it one step at a time? Just two friends enjoying each other's company." It almost felt wrong saying that to her when he knew what he felt was more than friendly toward her. But he wasn't ready to explore that. He just knew he wanted to spend more time with her.

She hesitated for a moment. "Okay," she said, not sounding completely convinced.

He smiled, ready to take any time she would give him. "Good. I'll pick you up Saturday at around four, if that's not too early. I'd like to take you out on the water."

Her eyes filled with excitement. "That would be perfect. I haven't been out on the water since I moved here."

"Get out of here. Seriously?"

She laughed. "Well, don't say it like that. Not everyone who lives at the beach owns a boat."

He grinned and picked up another balloon. "I don't. But Jonah has more boats than he knows what to do with. We'll take one of his."

"It's nice to know people."

"It really is. Now, how is the building coming along? Any more thoughts on it?"

She smiled again as she filled a balloon. "I rented it. I take possession tomorrow, actually, so when you pick me up, it will be there. I won't have much there with me but I'll have a few things to start out with. I'm excited. Mami, Birdie, Lila, and Doreen are going to help me. Rosie and your sister, Erin, want to help but I told them they have their own businesses to worry about right now and—"

"I'll come help you."

"Thanks, but actually, like I told them there isn't that much to move yet. I have a blowup mattress for now and the things people have given me. I'll be ordering a few things to have delivered and then start hitting resale shops tomorrow and hope to find enough cool things to fill my apartment. I'll start getting things in order. And I'm hoping I'll have the business open in a month."

"Wow. When you say you want to do something, you don't mess around."

She smiled. "You told me it was in good shape and I took you at your word, Fire Chief."

He liked her. Liked her a lot.

"You are bold. I don't see you as the type of person who hides behind things. Like that big bush at the dog park when you were avoiding me."

She seemed to tense and then picked up a fresh balloon and prepared it to be filled. "I have my moments." She let out a long breath and he thought she looked concerned and wondered what was on her mind.

"Brad, we're here to help." His mother's familiar voice sounded behind him. He turned to find his mom and dad smiling behind him.

"Mom. Dad. Glad you made it."

"Of course, we did. We wouldn't miss this. It's

too important." Maryetta Sinclair smiled brightly as she looked at Lulu. "Hello, you're Lulu Raintree, aren't you, the wonderful dog walker? The one who lost her apartment in that terrible fire last week." It wasn't a question but a statement.

Lulu stood, and held out her hand. "Yes, I am."

"Lulu, this is my mom and dad, Maryetta and Leo Sinclair."

She smiled that lovely smile that turned his insides to warm goo and made him feel...young again.

"It's so nice to meet you both. I'm grateful for Brad and his other wonderful crew of heroes for putting out the fire before it could hurt anyone or harm anyone else's things."

She smiled directly at him and he forgot everything but how that smile made him feel. As if he could stand there in that spot, looking at her forever.

"Brad, son."

He suddenly realized his mother must have said his name more than once and he hadn't heard her.

"I'm sorry, what?"

His mom smiled. "I was saying, this is a very

smart young woman. I like her." She smiled knowingly at him then at Lulu. "I like you. Anyone who recognizes how wonderful Brad is gets my highest regard. But, I'm so sorry you lost everything."

"I'm fine. I have everything I need right now—a coffeepot, a few changes of clothes, and a lot of good friends."

"Hey, Mom. Dad." Erin came up to them. "So, glad y'all are here. Can you come help me fix your famous cheese dip? I have it started, however, I've never made it and I'm just not sure if I'm doing it correctly."

"I'll be right there," she said but didn't follow Erin. Instead, she assessed him and Lulu for a moment, and Brad did not miss that gleam in her eyes. She had ideas forming that made him uncomfortable.

"Mom," Erin called, and finally his mother followed her. As she led his parents away Erin glanced over her shoulder and winked at him.

He loved his sister. He would give her a hug later.

"Erin gave you a break." He hitched a brow at Lulu making her laugh softly.

"Thank goodness. I saw a gleam in your mom's eyes that made me a little uncomfortable."

He grimaced. "Me too. She's pushing really hard for her kids to get married and give her grandchildren. We are all grateful to Adam and Rosie for their upcoming wedding. Takes some of the pressure off. Although I've already told them not to count me in on marriage or grandkids any time soon."

"I know how you feel."

Lila and Doreen passed by, each carrying what looked like about six pie boxes each.

"It's almost time for this party to start, you two," Lila said. "I see folks parking down the street and heading this way."

"Thanks, Lila," Brad called. "I better go make a round and see if I'm needed anywhere. I'll be back, hopefully. But just in case we both get so busy we don't get to talk again, don't forget about Saturday. I'll be there at four."

She smiled. "I'll be ready."

CHAPTER ELEVEN

Rosie was watching the line of people ready to buy a plate of spaghetti to support the fire department when she felt Adam come up behind her and slip his arms around her.

"Are you ready for a break," he asked, placing a gentle kiss on her temple.

She wrapped her hands across his arms and nestled back into him, inhaling the scents of sandalwood and soap. He smelled delicious. "If you're ready to join me."

"I am. The desserts are basically serve yourself so

I'm assuming you don't need to stand here with them, and I think everything I could possibly help with is all done so we are free to enjoy the day."

"Perfect." She turned her head to kiss his jaw. She still couldn't believe that she was marrying this amazing man. Her heart galloped like a wild mustang on open beach every time she thought about it. Her dreams were coming true and she couldn't wait to exchange vows with him. She still couldn't believe she had been blessed with a second chance at life and love. And eventually children.

He took her hand and walked with her to get into the line. She couldn't help noticing how at ease he seemed now compared to when he'd first come back to town.

"Doctor Sinclair." A woman carrying a baby approached them. Her name was Jenna and she came into the bakery sometimes. "I just wanted to bring Elsa over for you to see. She is so much better. Thank you so much for treating her last week." She looked from Adam to smile at Rosie. "Your fiancé is a wonderful doctor." Rosie smiled in agreement.

Adam took the compliment with a nod and humble smile as he peered at the baby girl wrapped in the baby blanket. "Hi there," he said and the baby's gaze riveted to his face and a tiny smile appeared.

"Her breathing has been so much better since the breathing treatments."

"Good, her color looks good. And she's very responsive," he said as the baby grasped the finger he held out to her. "How's her appetite?"

"She's eating like a little horse."

"Good. If she shows any signs of a relapse please bring her back in."

"I will. Thanks so much, it's nice seeing both of you."

"You too," Rosie said and looked at her man. "You look so at home right now. You seem to really have adapted to the slower lifestyle of family practice versus the stress of the trauma units."

"I have. I never thought I'd adapt to family practice in a rural town. But I have. But mostly, I've adapted to being around you, Rosie."

The look of love in his eyes sent her pulse soaring.

"I feel the same way."

"I need to talk to you." Taking her hand he tugged her out of line and walked quickly around the outer edge of the firehouse. It was quieter here but he didn't stop there. Instead, he led her along the length of the building and then on the backside where there was only an exit door to the alley he stopped and pulled her into his arms and kissed her.

"What are you doing?" She chuckled against his lips, enjoying the feel of his kiss and the luxurious feel of specialness that came over her when he held her like this.

He didn't say anything for a long moment as he continued kissing her. Finally, he pulled away and stared at her. "I'm kissing my fiancée in private, in case you haven't figured that out yet." He stared deep into her eyes as he took both her hands in his.

She started to wonder suddenly if something was wrong. "Adam?"

His dimples showed and his eyes softened. "Rosie, I know we've been saying we're going to take our time and come up with a date for the wedding. But, I want you to know, that I'm ready to marry you right here and now. I will wait as long as you want, but I just needed to tell you that I'm ready. I'm happy, and settled and there is no going back for me. I like what I'm doing, and I'm not going back to trauma. That means you can relax about me. I know what I want and it's to stay right here and grow old with you."

She swallowed hard, as her dreams came even closer. "You're sure?"

"Look, Mom stopped me earlier and told me she'd been trying to get you to commit to a date for the wedding and that you continue to hesitate because you want to give me enough time to come to grips with what happened. She's anxious and by no means do I want you setting a date just to please my mother. But I don't want you not setting one because you're worried about me not being ready." Lifting her hands to his lips he kissed her fingers. "I'm ready anytime you say."

Rosie nearly melted right there. "Oh, Adam. I just didn't want to rush you but I'm so ready to be your wife." Tears sprang to her eyes.

"How about tonight? I can have plane tickets to

Vegas in an hour."

She bit back a startled laugh. "Not that ready. I could never do that to your family. Or mine…could I?"

"This is about you and me." Humor and temptation mixed together in his expression. Tempting her.

Tempting her so very much. Could she do this?

On Saturday, Lulu was ready and waiting when Brad came to pick her up for their date. The firehouse fundraiser had been fun and he'd been right; they'd barely had time to talk to each other after the mass of supporters showed up. He had been busy and it had been nice watching him in action and seeing how much the town supported their firemen.

He had surprised her that morning by showing up to help gather all the pieces of furniture that she'd found and brought them up the stairs to her new apartment. He'd gone home after she was settled, then came back to pick her up for their date.

"You clean up real nice." He grinned down at her.

"I like that pink blouse on you."

She had hoped the pink sleeveless top wasn't too bright with her hair but she loved bright colors and had decided to wear it. "Thank you. It's one of the things someone gave me. I'm still amazed by everyone's generosity. I could go shopping but I really like wearing the things everyone gave me. I find it comforting."

"Did I tell you that I like you? I like the way you think."

He had told her that and she liked hearing it again.

When they got to Jonah's Boat Rentals, he met them on the dock. He was handsome, with his lean, tanned face and slightly long hair.

"I've got my favorite boat ready for you two."

"Did they deliver my order?" Brad placed a hand on the curve of her lower back and let her go ahead of him, down the dock behind Jonah. She liked the feel of his light touch. She liked him too much.

The boat was not small, but then, what did she know about boats? There were two engines and places to sit in the front or in the back or next to the driver.

And there was a tiny boat tied to the side.

Excitement filled her as Brad stepped from the dock into the boat then turned, smiling, and held out his hand to her.

"Take it easy, until you get your sea legs beneath you."

"That may take a little while. I haven't been on a boat in a very long time."

"It comes back to you. You'll do fine."

"And don't worry," Jonah said. "Brad is an excellent captain. You'll be safe."

She wondered whether he said that because her expression gave away a nervousness she didn't feel. Actually, she had trusted Brad instantly. And these days, trust on so many levels was hard for her. Especially on a personal level. *Be careful*, her inner voice warned. *Tread lightly where he is concerned.*

"I'm getting the feeling that Brad is good at anything he does."

Jonah nodded. "Yep, that about sums him up in a nutshell. The man was born that way. But he doesn't take it for granted. He works hard to make sure he gets better at it and stays that way."

"I'm glad you threw that in," Brad said from where he was checking out the screen beside the steering wheel and levers. "I wouldn't want you to think I'm just a loafer."

"No one would ever think that." Jonah laughed and untied the rope at the front of the boat.

"If you're ready, take this seat. And here..." Brad picked up the life vest from the passenger seat. "Put this on."

She slipped it on and clipped the connectors.

He moved close and tugged them, testing them, and smiled at her. "All set. Here we go."

Her pulse had kicked up and she nodded. "Let's have some fun," she said, and was so very glad she'd found her confident self where he was concerned. At least for now, she was not a bumbling mess.

He paused, holding the straps to her vest and looking at her, causing her pulse to feel dangerously high. And then he let go and turned to the controls and turned the key. The engines roared to life.

Jonah tossed the rope into the front of the boat

then pushed off with his shoe. He moved to the other rope, released it and waved. "You kids have fun." He grinned and held his hand up.

She waved and sank to the seat as Brad pulled back on the lever that she assumed meant full speed ahead and they sped through the waters toward the horizon. She glanced back and saw that Jonah grew tiny on the boat dock quickly. She turned back to face the front of the boat, to watch the horizon coming at her in fast motion and to take in the knowledge that she and Brad had just left everything behind them in that moment. It might only be for a moment but for the here and now, she felt only exhilaration with the wind in her hair, the sun on her skin, and when she looked at Brad, his eyes smiled at her, dancing with the waves as they crashed through them with the power of the large engines driving them forward.

Bliss. Pure bliss.

In this moment, she let the power of what she felt take over. She didn't worry about not being able to trust her heart to anyone. That would come later, when she returned to solid ground again. She didn't worry about his record of never sticking around in a relationship, even if the woman was gorgeous and sexy, which she was not. She didn't worry about a whole host of things she could be worrying about where she and Brad were concerned. She just smiled at him, leaned back in her seat and let the bliss take over.

"There," Brad said, spotting a pod of porpoises.

"Awesome!" She swiveled the chair for a better look, watching as two sprang from the water momentarily. "I love this." She glanced over her shoulder at Brad. He was smiling. "Thank you for bringing me out to see this."

"No thank you needed. I'm glad you came. There goes another one."

She turned back to see the athletic mammal practically dance across the water, before the group headed away from them. She turned her chair back toward Brad. "That was really cool. Do you spend a lot of time on the water?" She was curious about him.

"As much as I can. But, to be honest, it's been awhile. I haven't brought anyone out with me even longer than that."

His confession pleased her more than she wanted it to. Knowing that he had brought her here where he clearly enjoyed being and he hadn't brought other women, at least not in a long time, gave her a warm, fuzzy feeling all over.

She bit her lip. Trepidation eased into her, messing with her contented feeling. She was not getting serious. She was just having a good time with a great guy.

A guy you've been obsessed with, girlfriend.

True.

"See that island there in the distance?"

She ignored the niggling voice. "Yes, I see it. It looks great. It doesn't look inhabited."

"It's not. But it's about to be."

Her gaze shot to him. "What?"

He laughed. "I've got dinner ready and waiting for me to float it over and unpack it."

"Are you kidding me?" She laughed, startled.

His eyes twinkled. "I surprised you, didn't I?"

"Completely surprised me. I'm overwhelmed, actually."

He slowed the boat and then eased it toward a

small cove with a white sandy beach and some low growing bushes. A single palm tree stood at a steep angle, as if it had survived storms and even hurricanes and had come through still standing.

The water was shallow now, and like all the water off the coast of Sunset Bay, she was realizing, it was as clear as ocean water could be.

He pushed a button. "Anchor is down." Moments later, he pulled the small boat over for her and helped her step into it and sit down. It was then that she noticed the cooler as he picked it up and set it in the boat with her before he took the other seat and untied the small boat from the larger one.

"I wondered what this boat was for," she said.

"I didn't want you to have to swim to shore." He grinned.

"Thank you very much." She pulled her gaze from him and focused on the shore as they motored toward it.

"Nothing like these little skiffs to get you around." He drove it right up on shore and then they climbed out.

"You're right. What a fun little boat."

"I thought you would like it. Give me a moment and I'll have dinner all set up."

"I can help-"

"No, this is my treat."

Within moments, he'd unpacked a large blanket and several containers of food then motioned toward the blanket.

"Here, have a seat. I hope you like my choices."

Still in shock, she sank onto the blanket, a smile permanently plastered to her face. "I don't think there is anything you could do right now that I wouldn't like. This…" She paused, truly overwhelmed. "Brad, this is just lovely."

He just smiled. "Actually, you're lovely."

The man was making points with everything he said or did. "Now I'm not sure what you're up to, buster."

He laughed. "I'm hoping to impress you." He opened the foil-covered metal container and there was a plate. "Sautéed snapper with lemongrass, served with rice cake and asparagus. And for dessert, your choice of triple-layer chocolate cake or cheesecake with raspberry glaze."

Her mouth watered and she was speechless. She swallowed hard, trying not to tear up. This was romantic and amazing. "No one has ever gone to this much trouble or preparation for me before."

He set the plate on the blanket in front of her. "As far as I'm concerned, they messed up."

Brad saw the emotion in Lulu's eyes and his heart clenched as he sat down and got his own plate out. She had looked at him as if he had just treated her better than she'd ever been treated before and he just thought that was a shame. Protective feelings for her had kicked in like he'd never felt before…not even with Katie.

The thought hit him like a freight train. *He had feelings for Lulu. Real feelings.*

"You ready to eat?" he asked, needing something to say as he processed his feelings.

"Yes. I can't wait."

They ate in silence for a few minutes as the sun sparkled over the water and began to lower on the horizon.

They made small talk and laughed. When the meal was over, he took her hand and they walked down the tiny private beach, enjoying the feel of the water on their feet and the soft glow of the sun.

Lulu had grown quiet and his heart thundered like nothing he'd ever felt before as he stopped walking, faced her and stared at her with wonder. *How had this happened?* Her huge eyes held his and then, with a need he couldn't deny, he gently took her face in his hands and lowered his lips to hers.

Her lips parted and she kissed him back as his heart hammered. In that moment, with the sun beginning to lower to the water's edge, he came to grips with the fact that he was falling in love with Lulu.

He'd never planned to risk his heart.

All the way back to the boat dock, Brad kept thinking about the feelings crowding through him. Smothering him, clawing at him and sending him spinning.

What had he done?

CHAPTER TWELVE

Lulu had kissed him. He'd kissed her.

She still couldn't think straight. Could barely breathe. They were almost back to the boat dock. She should be able to breathe by now. But she couldn't. Couldn't process what was going on inside her head.

Inside her heart.

Her heart pounded, her pulse rushed in her ears, and her thoughts scrambled as the boat pulled to the dock. She slid a glance at Brad. He was grim-faced. *Did he regret the kiss as much as she did?*

He had to. He had practically run to pack things

up, saying they needed to beat the darkness. She'd been glad, needing an excuse to be busy herself. They'd stowed everything in record time and then she'd climbed on to the boat before he could even think about offering her a helping hand. She'd grabbed her life jacket and had the snaps closed before he was on board.

He'd said something about her needing to watch the beautiful sunset, which she had gratefully done because it meant facing away from him and watching the back of the boat rather than anything forward. Saving her from being tempted to glance at him.

Probably saving him from having to meet her gaze, because something told her he didn't want to do that as much as she didn't want to do it.

When the front of the boat was tied off, she climbed out and waited for him to tie the back of the boat to the dock. The place was closed; it was now dark and they'd finished the trip in with lights on the boat. They walked to the truck in silence.

"Thanks. It was a great trip," she said as they made it to the truck.

"You're welcome. I'm glad you could come along."

Was he? Was she?

He opened the Jeep door for her and she climbed in, ignoring the scent of his aftershave.

It was hard to ignore. But not long after, he dropped her off at the apartment, where they had an awkward exchange at the front door. She thanked him quickly and then escaped inside before he could say much more than goodnight.

Brad stopped by Adam's beach cottage hoping to catch his brother. He felt like maybe he needed to talk to someone and since Adam had recently become engaged maybe he would understand some of the emotions he was feeling. But the lights were off at Adam's and his truck was gone. He noticed that Rosie's place looked dark too and decided they must be on a date.

The moonlight and ocean were glistening across the beach from the cottages as he tucked his hands into his pockets and walked across Adam's small back yard to the beach. He'd always done his thinking at the beach when it was quiet. But tonight he didn't have any answers. He just kept having thoughts of holding Lulu. What if he gave her his heart and she walked away. Maybe not immediately but later down the road, after he felt secure in her love. Like he'd felt with Katie only to have his world yanked out from under him?

He'd gotten over Katie, but Lulu was different. He knew he might never get over her leaving if he were to give into the love for her that burned inside him.

Shaking his head he turned and went back to his Jeep. He needed to go home and try and move on with his life. He couldn't do this and he knew it.

What had he been thinking?

On Sunday morning, Lulu had no dogs to walk, as everyone managed without her on this one day of the week. She thought about going to church but just didn't want to be around people right now. Especially knowing that there would be endless questions that she was not ready to answer. Instead, she got in her car and drove the two blocks to the bakery, thinking maybe Rosie would be there and she could talk to her friend. Rosie wouldn't push or pry and would probably just be a good friend and sounding board for her to talk to and try and make sense of the feelings she was feeling. But the bakery was closed.

She stood outside the door, cupped her hands together and stared through the glass to see if there was movement inside that she was missing. But no, the bakery was dark and clearly closed for the day. For a few minutes, she stopped thinking about herself and wondered where Rosie was. Not ready to see anyone or to go back to her bare apartment she got back into her vehicle and drove out of town. She was going to find a big weekend trade sale and walk and wander around all day if she needed to. She might find some neat things for her new apartment or her business while at the same time just disappear for a few hours.

Running away seemed to be her thing these days. But right now she didn't care, she just needed to be alone and gather her thoughts. Tomorrow she would get busy and throw herself into getting her new business up and running and hopefully have answers to all the questions her friends were going to ask.

On Monday morning feeling like she had a plan, Lulu headed to Rosie's for a muffin and coffee before picking up Spaz and Sussi-Q. She needed fortification before those two little devil dogs tried to do her in.

On her outing the day before she had had found some end tables and a chair for her apartment along with some dishes and other items she'd needed. She had been able to get the tables in her backseat and the chair fit into her trunk once she left the trunk lid open and tied it with a string. It had been a good trip and allowed her time to think. To refocus on getting back into her normal routine. Things had just been upside down since the fire.

"Good morning," Rosie exclaimed the moment she walked through the door. She smiled like sunshine on a storm filled day. "How did your weekend go?

Mine was fantastic."

Rosie's eyes were sparkling and she just looked extra happy. "It was...good. I came by early yesterday and missed you. Did you take the day off?" she asked. She was usually Rosie's first client and they'd struck up their friendship that way with early morning conversations. Those conversations had helped Lulu in more ways than Rosie knew.

Now, Rosie blushed, and looked almost bashful for an instant. "I did take a day off. Actually, I went with Adam."

"I thought you might have." She waited for Rosie to say more but she didn't. Instead, she fixed Lulu's coffee and then slid it across the counter to her.

"Which muffin do you want today? The regular?"

"Yes. Orange marmalade is my comfort food." She said the comfort food remark before she thought better of it.

But, too late it alerted Rosie who peered closer at her. "Why do you need comfort food? Did something happen on your date? Did it not go well?"

"It went okay. It's fine." She did not like lying.

And when Rosie came around the counter to face her, she knew Rosie didn't believe her.

"Something tells me there is more to this than you're letting on."

"Okay, okay, so I'm lying," she burst out feeling some relief letting the truth out. "Please keep this to yourself, but he kissed me…*kissed me* and it scared the fire out of me."

Rosie sighed. "I think that's wonderful."

"Wonderful? No, no I don't think so. I can't do that again."

"Lulu, please give this a chance. Love can be scary after what you've been through, and him too. You both were stood up at the altar. And you lost your brother. Adam says Brad looked really happy at the fundraiser with you. He said he couldn't keep his eyes off of you the whole time they were setting up tables and chairs. And then he watched you two together blowing up balloons and he knew his brother was feeling something again. He was so excited."

Lulu stared at Rosie. "I just don't see it. I mean, look at me, you know the bombshells he normally dates. He's just spending time with me until he moves on."

Rosie's mouth dropped open and her eyes widened in disbelief. "You are beautiful."

"I'm short. I'm dumpy, compared to the long, lean women I've seen him with. I just think he has a thing for redheads with long legs and toned muscles. The red hair has him confused right now. And then being nice to me after the fire."

"Lulu, stop. That is not so. You are much more than your gorgeous hair."

She took a big bite of her orange marmalade muffin, needing something to help her hide the emotions raging through her. But she was so uptight that the sweet muffin seemed to grow in her mouth.

"My hair is the color of carrots," she mumbled. "Or this orange muffin." She held it up.

"And the color is unique and as delicious looking as my muffins taste."

Hardly. She took a drink of coffee and tried to gather her emotions. "I have to go."

Rosie stepped in front of her. "Wait. Please, I need

to tell you something. Lulu you've stopped believing in fairy tales because you nearly married a frog the first time and not your prince. Now, I believe your prince has come along and you just can't let yourself believe. Please don't close your heart. Do you know what I did this weekend?"

Lulu shook her head, wanting to go but not wanting to be so rude to her sweet friend who was only trying to make her feel better.

"Adam and I eloped."

Had she heard her correctly? "What? No, you didn't."

Rosie's expression was jubilant. "We did. At the fire station, he asked me if I wanted to and, well, you know I almost died and at first I thought no, we couldn't do that and disappoint his family, his mother especially, but he convinced me that this was about he and I." Tears sprang to Rosie's eyes. "I couldn't resist him."

Lulu threw her arms around her. "I am so happy for you. You deserve this so much."

Rosie sniffed and smiled so sweetly at her. "Thank

you. But, Lulu, so do you. That's why I'm sharing this with you. Please give yourself another chance at love. Please, please, please, don't give up on Brad or yourself. Don't shut him out."

"Oh, Rosie, I don't know."

"Life is short, my sweet friend. I know just how short it can be. Don't judge Brad by his past. Or your past. You ran away to help deal with your heartbreak. He stayed here and because he was lonely and wasted a lot of time with other women while waiting on you to arrive."

Lulu realized that she wanted to believe this. She really did. She blinked back tears. "I need to go. And just so you know, I'm not running away again. I'm staying here even if it means seeing Brad every day and knowing we weren't meant to be."

"Good, and don't say that, give it a chance." Rosie smiled broadly again. "And please keep my elopement to yourself for a little while. We haven't told his parents yet. That's happening tonight."

That meant Rosie would see Brad. "I'll do that. I'm so happy for you. But please don't say anything about this to Brad."

"I won't."

She held Rosie's gaze, and felt she meant what she said. She left the bakery feeling happiness for Rosie but still confused about her own emotions but at least knowing her secrets were safe with Rosie.

She spent the rest of the day hiring painters, and ordering kennels and other supplies she was going to need, including doggie playground equipment. She did her normal dog walking in between getting things organized. It helped to have so much to do. She called a fence builder Birdie recommended to come and build a fence around the open lot. And all the while she was so busy, her heart was fickle and silly and aching.

Her friends came to help and to find out firsthand about how her date with Brad—which, she decided quickly was the main reason for helping. Mami, Doreen, Lila, and Birdie were good friends but they were also nosey little sweethearts. Sneaky too she suspected.

"Now, ladies, don't get your hopes up on this being a match made in heaven because I hate to disappoint you but neither he nor I are ready for a relationship. At least not one with merit."

They all stared at her like she'd just spoken in a foreign language, pausing in their various jobs around the room of dusting or sweeping.

"But why?" Doreen asked, timidly. "You two are perfect for each other."

For Doreen to be the first to speak it meant she really felt strongly about this. Lulu wanted to hug her.

"Yes, why wouldn't you be ready for a relationship with him?" Lila asked and the other two echoed her.

"Look, there is more to my story than you know." Did she want to come clean about her past? It was suddenly exhausting living with her secrets. Especially with the four ladies who had been nothing but good to her.

"I have had a feeling all wasn't right in your past," Mami said, looking sympathetically at her. "Anything we can help with?"

"Actually, there isn't anything you can help with really, but, I'd like to explain. You four ladies have been such blessings to me."

"What is it dear?" Lila asked, coming over as the others gathered close.

"I have a connection to Brad because I was abandoned at the altar too. My fiancé decided at the last moment that my bridesmaid would make a better wife and they ran off together."

Gasps rolled from their mouths like a wave.

"Not you too?" Mami asked.

"That's ridiculous," Birdie snapped. "What an idiot he must have been. But all is well for you because Brad Sinclair is not an idiot. He might be having trouble getting his head on straight after going through the same thing, but an idiot he is not. And he is going to come to his senses. Mark my words, young lady."

"It's not that simple, Birdie. I'm confused too. And leery also."

"Well, maybe we need a yoga session," Lila said, looking seriously at her. "To clear your head and get the blood pumping back in there. Because clearly you haven't yet realized you dodged a bad deal and have now run slap into a great deal."

Leave it to Lila. If only yoga would fix this she would be on it right away.

"Tell us the rest," Doreen said. "Because I think there is more, isn't there?"

"Yes, there is." With that she proceeded to tell them about her brother's death and then her dog and then her decision to leave town. She told them about the date too. It was as if once she'd started talking she couldn't stop. At last she came to the kiss and her emotions and his sudden quietness.

"You haven't heard from him?" Lila asked, in disbelief.

Mami's face wrinkled up in disbelief. "The boy hasn't called you after taking you out? Or come by? For heaven's sake, that is ridiculous."

"No. The truth is that I'm busy and he probably is too. But there is more, I think we both just realized we couldn't go forward. I just don't think I have the trust inside me to give to anyone ever again."

"Maybe it's worse than we suspected and we need

to give that boy a refresher course on how to treat a lady after a date," Lila declared, standing with her hands on her hips near the doggy obstacle course. "I mean, really. I am so disappointed in him. I thought for sure this was different from his other, well, you know, escapades since Katie walked out on him."

Birdie looked disgruntled. "I did too. I wouldn't have pushed you to go out with him if I had known he was going to run again."

Her heart was running away with her at the moment and like she'd been doing since the date she closed herself off to the hurt she felt every time she thought of him.

She had hoped she would be different for him? She had hoped in her subconscious that she would be different, that she would be the one he could fall for? Even if she was afraid to believe it.

"It's okay, friends. Really. He has gone through something very traumatic. I did too, as you now know. I can tell you that it's hard to overcome betrayal. I think I'm fine with things the way they stand. So please don't say anything to him. Please."

Doreen, who had become very quiet walked over and wrapped her arms around Lulu. "You are brave," she whispered. "You'll be fine." And then she walked away and left Lulu determined to be just that—brave.

She would get through this.

"What do you mean you haven't spoken to her since you took her out?" Erin asked Brad at the family dinner at her parents' home.

"I haven't, Erin. I know that upsets you but that's all I can do. She barely spoke to me that night after I took her home. She's fine with things the way they are."

"That sounds wrong," Jonah said. "I saw you two leaving in the boat and you both looked happy. Excited even. What happened to make such a turnaround when you arrived back at my place?"

"Yeah," Adam asked. "It just sounds off."

Brad gave Adam a you-aren't-helping glare. Adam was holding Rosie's hand and they looked at each other and Brad thought there was silent messaging passing between them. He'd thought they had been about to tell the family something prior to Erin's sudden questioning him about his date.

Rosie took a deep breath. "She came by the shop this morning for a muffin and her morning coffee. But she looks really sad. You should go see her."

Brad looked away and caught his mother studying him. His father too. This family meal was not the best thing for a time like this. A time when he was trying to just get by.

"What did you do?" his mother asked. "You look guilty, Brad. When you were a little boy and would pull stunts or pranks on your brothers, I could always tell when it was you. And you look just like that right now."

"Your mother is right, son."

He grimaced and wiped emotion from his face but everyone in the room saw it. *Not good.*

"You did something," Erin said. "Brad, what did you do? Did you kiss her?"

His gaze shot to her and he knew then and there that he was caught. Red-handed like a kid with his hand in the cookie jar.

"Okay, okay. I kissed her. And when I kissed her, I knew that I shouldn't have."

"Why? How would you know that?" Maryetta Sinclair asked him.

He looked at his mother, wishing he could lie to her but knowing he'd never in his adult life done that...and never would. Maybe it was best to get it out in the open. "I didn't know until that moment that I had feelings for her, okay? I never planned to risk my heart again. And I won't. That's why it's over."

"Son." Leo stepped out of the kitchen and came to stand before him. "I'm saying this as your dad, as your friend, and as a man a whole lot older than you, with a lot more life experience. So listen to me. That is about the stupidest excuse I've ever heard for not letting yourself be happy. You got hurt and if you lay down in this and wallow in it for the rest of your life, then, son, you are not the man I've come to respect and know. You are strong. You are a man every person in this community looks up to and this is wrong. Wrong, mostly for you.

"Your mother is the most wonderful thing that ever happened to me. I don't know if you know it but I got stood up at the altar. I don't talk about it but it was the best thing that ever happened to me. A blessing in disguise and I praise God every day for it. Your mother came along a few years after that and I am thankful. I took one look at her and knew we were meant for each other. In that moment, I never thought about that other woman again. Only as a blessing. Maybe you need to start thinking the same way. Because, son, Katie wasn't right for you. And if you're still carrying a torch for her, then you're in the wrong."

"I don't carry a torch for her."

"Then you're running scared," Adam said and pulled Rosie close and kissed her temple.

He sighed. "Yes, I'm running scared."

"You walk away from this, you'll be running for the rest of your life and most likely regret it in your old age."

He looked around and knew his family was right. But, she might not look at it that way. "But I'm not the only one running scared, I think. I think Lulu is too."

191

"Adam," Rosie said, her voice sounding strained. Everyone stared at her as she looked at Adam and nodded.

"We have something to confess. And before you all get upset hear me out. Brad, you need to get over your past and move on. And you need to move whatever mountain it takes to get that done. For your happiness and for Lulu's. I have it under good authority, and am unable to reveal my sources who are sworn to secrecy, but I think Lulu's happiness hangs in the balance right now and is contingent on your next move." He smiled at Rosie.

Brad's heart had started hammering recklessly. Could it be true? Had Rosie and Lulu talked? Was Rosie sworn to secrecy? He started for the door.

"Hold up, not so fast," Adam called. "Rosie and I have an announcement."

He turned back to them. "What?"

"We moved a mountain Early Sunday morning in Vegas."

"Vegas," Maryetta gasped, her eyes wide as she looked from Adam to Rosie. Both were now smiling jubilantly.

"You got married?" he asked, knowing it was true. He strode back to them and engulfed them both in a hug before the rest of his family had time to react. "I am shocked and thrilled at the same time. You sly dog you, Adam."

"You two," his mother was crying, "I am so mad at you and happy at the same time. Oh goodness, I can't believe it." She took Brad's place hugging the newlyweds and then looked at him. "Go see your Lulu."

Adam grinned. "Go make your happy day happen."

To the sound of cheers for him and congratulations for Adam and Rosie, Brad strode through the house and burst outside feeling like he was moving in slow motion.

He needed to get to Lulu. He needed her.

He just prayed she needed him too.

CHAPTER THIRTEEN

Lulu was in the dog park, refusing to look at the firehouse, when, out of the corner of her eye, she saw a fast-approaching yellow Jeep. She ducked behind the bush and held her breath, wondering if she could make a run for it across the dog park and to her apartment. She hoped he hadn't seen her. She was a mess.

Tires screeched and she spun to see the Jeep slam to a halt just outside the gate of the park. Brad sprang from the Jeep and jogged around the front and, to her startled surprise, he placed both hands on the top of the metal fence and vaulted over, basically landing a few feet in front of her.

"Brad," she gasped.

"I'm an idiot," he said. "A big, blundering idiot. Lulu, I kissed you because I couldn't help myself. I kissed you because it was what my heart wanted to do and then I shut down. I let my brain tell my heart what I was going to do and that was the wrong thing for me. My family helped wake me up. I've been living in a shuttered life, pretending that I wanted to be alone for the rest of my life, and I don't. Until you came out of the shadows and touched me, I was just a shadow myself. A fool. You and I both have been hurt. I get that you know how I felt and I know how you felt.

"But Lulu, I don't care about all that now. It was a blessing. My dad pointed that out to me. And he is absolutely right. I don't think of Katie any longer at all. I only think of you. I think of you all the time. I want you. I need you and I am hoping that you might feel the same way about me. I'm praying you feel the same way about me." He dropped to his knee.

Lulu started to cry. She was a ball of neverending tears these days. "I do," she whispered, through the tears. "I really do, Brad. I love you."

He smiled, then took her hand. "Then let's do this together. Because I love you, Lulu Raintree, and I want to see you walk down that aisle to me and say I do as you become my wife. I'll say I do for the rest of my life, with every breath I breathe if you will marry me."

Fairy tales were real. Lulu threw her arms around his neck. "I do. I do. I always do."

He grabbed her up and twirled her around, laughing with delight that filled her with the most amazing satisfaction she'd ever known.

"You are my hero," she whispered and kissed him.

He chuckled and said against her lips, "You are my hero—exactly what I've been longing for my entire life."

"I agree," she said. And as he stopped twirling her and her feet touched the ground again, she knew her heart would never touch the ground again. It was forever his.

And for the first time since her heart had been crushed, she knew she would forever be grateful for that day that had sent her running to Sunset Bay.

And she knew her brother would be more than happy for her.

EPILOGUE

Erin stood at the wedding cake table holding the cake knife that she had just sliced at least two hundred slices of cake with so far at Adam and Rosie's wedding reception. Everyone wanted to share in Adam and Rosie's happy occasion. Her brothers were the talk of the town. Adam and Rosie running off to Vegas and the adventure they'd had there getting married. And Brad and Lulu getting engaged. It had been a week since Adam and Rosie's announcement and Brad asking Lulu to be his wife and the buzz around town had not stopped.

She loved it.

"I knew they were meant for each other from the moment they laid eyes on each other, "Lila exclaimed across the cake table to Erin.

"Are you talking about Adam and Rosie or Brad and Lulu?" Birdie chuckled.

"Both." Lila giggled. "Those Sinclair boys didn't stand a chance against Rosie and Lulu."

"No they did not," Mami agreed and smiled toward Erin's brothers, Tate and Jonah. "Those over there are looking a little worried I think. For two Sinclair men to fall in love in two months... I bet they're worried there is something in the water."

Doreen giggled. "There might be."

Erin hid her smile and sliced another piece of buttercream cake. She knew Tate was a long way away from that but Jonah just needed the right woman to come along. At least she thought so.

She, Tate, and Cassie were nowhere near ready for love. She had too much on her plate with the Bed and Breakfast and Tate, who knew where he was going to be on any given day and the same with Cassie.

"I'm so happy," her mother said, as she and Cassie walked over from the punch line. She handed Erin a cup of punch.

"I'm happy for you," Mami said, all smiles. "I know you want grandchildren."

"I do. I'm hoping soon."

"Don't rush them. They look so happy," Cassie said, lifting her ever-present camera and snapping a shot of the two happy couples dancing on the dance floor.

"That's right, no need to rush them." Birdie grinned. "But little ones would be fun."

The song ended and her brothers headed their way. Erin felt a sudden twinge in her heart looking at them. She wanted what they had, just not yet. Maybe if things went well at the B&B she would be ready next year. Or the next year.

"Ladies, what are you all looking so happy about?" Brad asked, stopping to stare at the row of older women watching them and then he cocked his head toward his mother. "Has my mother been instigating trouble?"

That got laughs.

"No, we're just talking about the future."

Adam hugged Rosie to him. "I think she's talking babies again."

Rosie blushed and her eyes twinkled like a million stars. "Maryetta, we're trying to make you happy."

"Really!" Maryetta exclaimed.

"I figured that." Birdie chuckled. "I had a feeling Rosie was longing for a baby."

"I am. I can't wait."

"And I'm rooting for the two of you to fill that gap for me," Brad drawled. "Me and Lulu aren't going to rush it."

"We have to get married first. And we don't have a date yet," Lulu said. "But I will be a great aunt when the time comes."

"Me too," Cassie said.

"Hey, me too," Erin called. She would love to be an aunt. Her phone rang and she laid down the knife, licked the icing from her finger and then pulled the phone from her pocket. "I'll be right back."

Happy for her family, she strode off to the side of

the pavilion and accepted the call. It was her booking agent. She hoped it was for someone to fill the blank spaces she had on her upcoming calendar. There were far too many open spots. Getting her B&B started was proving to be harder than she'd believed.

"Hello," she said, and listened as the agent came on.

"Erin, we have a very special client looking to book a room for a two-month period of time."

"Two months?" Could she be so lucky?

"Yes, they came across your place but they have specific needs. Could possibly extend the stay to three months if the place works out for them. It will mean extra work on your part to accommodate their requirements."

She tried to keep her voice steady. "I'm sure for someone wanting to pay me for two months I can do about anything to accommodate them." She meant it too.

"Well, they want to rent your third floor for that time period."

"My honeymoon suite?"

"Yes. I know your ads are pushing your B&B as a honeymoon destination with that lovely room but this is a writer. A very well-known author's agent thinks your upper room is perfect for her client to work in for a couple of months. She believes he will love it."

"He? As in who?" Her curiosity clamored for information,

"Nash Bond."

Erin nearly choked. "*The* Nash Bond?"

"Yes. Your silence is needed in this. He's looking for a retreat to finish his latest novel. Part of the requirements is that you tell no one."

The man was one of the top selling intrigue authors and he'd had movies made of his work and had become a household name by the time he was thirty. She'd watched an interview with the guy not too long ago. He was dark-haired, gorgeous and worth who knew how much since he'd been listed in Forbes as one of the wealthiest authors out there and most eligible bachelor. And he was hard to deal with when he was working. She remembered that part clearly.

"Requirements? Anything you need, I can provide.

You know I pride myself on being the best hostess there is. But he can afford to rent a home, a mansion if he wanted. I don't completely understand."

"His agent thinks he needs his routine shaken up a bit. This is for your ears only, but he's in a slump. A block. And his agent thinks being holed up alone is not what he needs this time. Something about your honeymoon suite has caught the agent's eye and they are willing to pay for it. With the requirements included. What do you think?"

Erin needed this. With renovation cost exceeding what she'd first believed she needed the cash flow. She looked across the pavilion at her family and how happy they were and her heart squeezed tightly. She was happy for Adam and Rosie, Brad and Lulu. And this was what could make her happy. She'd been struggling to keep her rising stress to herself. And now, like a gift this Nash Bond was the answer she needed. Whatever his requirements were, or however hard to handle he might be, she was up for the challenge if it meant saving herself from the embarrassment of failure.

"I'm in. I'll do whatever's needed to make Mr.

Bond's stay at my B&B successful."

"Perfect. I told his agent you would say that. I'll let her know. And Erin," her booking agent paused. "Good luck. I think you might need it."

Erin stared at the phone, the agent's words ringing in her ear. "Well, I don't need luck," she muttered. She could do this. Nash Bond was going to have the best stay of his life at her B&B.

Because everything she had, very possibly, could be riding on that fact.

Don't miss LONGING FOR LOVE when Erin Sinclair meets the intriguing but demanding, Nash Bond. Will it be a disaster...or will love erupt from the fireworks these two ignite the moment they meet?

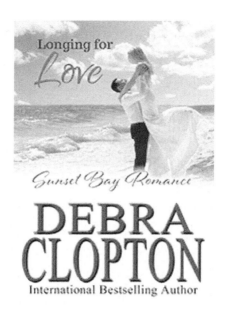

DEBRA CLOPTON

International Bestselling Author

Sometimes a dream might need a rewrite…

Erin Sinclair's dream of running a successful B&B is on shaky ground. Her tiny Inn is building a good reputation but needs more guest and more good reviews. When a New York Times bestselling author's agent books the honeymoon suite as a writing retreat it is an opportunity to put The Inn at Sunset Bay on the map. The Nash Bond is coming to her B&B for two months and Erin can hardly believe it. But he has a reputation of being hard to handle when he's in the midst of a book. And he's reclusive too. So what is he doing coming to her B&B? And what if she's unable to satisfy him? What if instead of a good review he gives her a terrible review?

Everything is on the line, is she up for the challenge? She has to be.

Nash Bond needs this book. He needs to get out of the slump he's in, but a year ago his life changed when he lost his adoptive father, his hero and the words that had once flowed without worry suddenly dried up in his grief. Now his agent is shaking things up by booking him a special room in a special place, her words, and she insist he give it a try. She reminds him his publisher is getting impatient. He knows everything is on the line. He doesn't like it at all and when he meets the gorgeous, but pushy B&B owner sparks fly. He's suddenly feeling things he's never felt before...but with his past he knows all too well that longing for love leaves a person open to pain thus he locked his heart away a long time ago and has no plans to change.

But on the shores of Sunset Bay can romance bloom? Can love heal a broken heart and give him a happily-ever-after he never thought he wanted? Or needed?

More Books by Debra Clopton

Sunset Bay Romance
Longing for Forever (Book 1)
Longing for a Hero (Book 2)
Longing for Love (Book 3)

Texas Brides & Bachelors
Heart of a Cowboy (Book 1)
Trust of a Cowboy (Book 2)
True Love of a Cowboy (Book 3)

New Horizon Ranch Series
Her Texas Cowboy (Book 1)
Rafe (Book 2)
Chase (Book 3)
Ty (Book 4)
Dalton (Book 5)
Treb (Book 6)
Maddie's Secret Baby (Book 7)
Austin (Book 8)

Cowboys of Ransom Creek
Her Cowboy Hero (Book 1)
The Cowboy's Bride for Hire (Book 2)
Cooper: Charmed by the Cowboy (Book 3)
Shane: The Cowboy's Junk-Store Princess (Book 4)
Vance: Her Second-Chance Cowboy (Book 5)
Drake: The Cowboy and Maisy Love (Book 6)
Brice: Not Quite Looking for a Family (Book 7)

Turner Creek Ranch Series
Treasure Me, Cowboy (Book 1)
Rescue Me, Cowboy (Book 2)
Complete Me, Cowboy (Book 3)
Sweet Talk Me, Cowboy (Book 4)

Texas Matchmaker Series
Dream With Me, Cowboy (Book 1)
Be My Love, Cowboy (Book 2)
This Heart's Yours, Cowboy (Book 3)
Hold Me, Cowboy (Book 4)
Be Mine, Cowboy (Book 5)
Marry Me, Cowboy (Book 6)
Cherish Me, Cowboy (Book 7)
Surprise Me, Cowboy (Book 8)
Serenade Me, Cowboy (Book 9)
Return To Me, Cowboy (Book 10)
Love Me, Cowboy (Book 11)
Ride With Me, Cowboy (Book 12)
Dance With Me, Cowboy (Book 13)

Windswept Bay Series
From This Moment On (Book 1)
Somewhere With You (Book 2)
With This Kiss (Book 3)
Forever and For Always (Book 4)
Holding Out For Love (Book 5)
With This Ring (Book 6)
With This Promise (Book 7)
With This Pledge (Book 8)
With This Wish (Book 9)
With This Forever (Book 10)
With This Vow (Book 11)

About the Author

Bestselling author Debra Clopton has sold over 2.5 million books. Her book OPERATION: MARRIED BY CHRISTMAS has been optioned for an ABC Family Movie. Debra is known for her contemporary, western romances, Texas cowboys and feisty heroines. Sweet romance and humor are always intertwined to make readers smile. A sixth generation Texan she lives with her husband on a ranch deep in the heart of Texas. She loves being contacted by readers.

Visit Debra's website at www.debraclopton.com

Sign up for Debra's newsletter at
www.debraclopton.com/contest/

Check out her Facebook at
www.facebook.com/debra.clopton.5

Follow her on Twitter at @debraclopton

Contact her at debraclopton@ymail.com

If you enjoyed reading *Longing for a Hero* I would appreciate it if you would help others enjoy this book, too.

Recommend it. Please help other readers find this book by recommending it to friends, reader's groups and discussion boards.

Review it. Please tell other readers why you liked this book by reviewing it on the retail site you purchased it from or Goodreads. If you do write a review, please send an email to debraclopton@ymail.com so I can thank you with a personal email. Or visit me at: www.debraclopton.com.

Made in the USA
Coppell, TX
23 June 2020

29256552R00118